Escaping Camp Ravensbrook

R. T. Johnson

Escaping Camp Ravensbrook

R. T. Johnson

ISBN:1517724716

Contents

PROLOGUE

The night's cold wind sent chills down Katrina's back. She went to close her window. Under her bedroom door, a bright light shone from the other room. She heard a scream. It sounded as if it came from the kitchen where her mother was preparing dinner. Her mother was cooking Katrina's favorites, fresh potatoes with broccoli and grilled beef. But, this night Katrina would not be eating any of it.

"HIDE!" her father called from the bottom of the stairs. They had practiced for this kind of thing. They knew it would happen. Her parents wanted more than anything to save Katrina.

Katrina hid. She covered herself in blankets and crawled under her bed. The necklace her father had given her was wrapped tightly in her fingers. It held power and blessings.

"Don't kill my wife!" She heard her father yell. A gunshot went off. It echoed throughout the house. Then came the scream. Katrina knew it was her mother's scream. She lay under her bed frozen. She heard the loud thud of her mother's body fall onto the hard wood floor. The glass from the cabinets shatter from the movement.

She heard her father cry. "Now you must kill me!" he demanded. "I fight for the Resistance and no matter how many of us you kill, we will win!" There was a second shot. And, a second thud. Katrina gasped for air. In a matter of minutes, her parents were gone, and she heard the whole thing.

"We'll need more bullets." She could hear the men

talking. Then they laughed. She heard them rummaging through the house.

What seemed like hours later, but was only several minutes, the murderers left. Her parents' bodies lay in pools of blood on the kitchen floor.

In disbelief and horror, Katrina packed quickly. She knew what she had to do. Her mother told her if they were ever taken, to go to her Aunt Lisa, her father's oldest sister. Her aunt would help her. She too was a secret member of the Resistance group. She was also a religious woman who held the same *powers* as Katrina. It was Aunt Lisa who taught her father *magic* and how to use the nature around them to make the world a better place. And, now Aunt Lisa had been teaching Katrina about the gift she was born with.

Katrina took her bag and went to the kitchen. She tried not to look at her parents as she went to the phone. She dialed the phone with trembling fingers. "They were killed," she said. Somehow, Katrina didn't cry. She didn't feel fearful. Instead, she just focused on the *now*. She could grieve for her family once she was safe.

Aunt Lisa took a moment to breathe. Katrina could hear the soft weak breath over the phone. She too focused on the present. "Then we are next," she said.

"Will they kill us too?" asked Katrina.

"We won't be killed. We will be taken though," her aunt said.

Before Katrina got to say another word to her aunt, the front door opened. A bright light filtered into the room.

"You," said a man behind the light. She could see his outline. He was big and tall and had the voice of a bear that was hungry for meat.

"Yes," Katrina said. She wished she wasn't standing near her parent's bodies.

"You are to come with me or you will be killed like your parents," he said.

There was no point in fighting. She dropped the phone and walked towards the light. The fifteen year old was placed in handcuffs and dragged to a large truck. She was then pushed inside.

Katrina looked out the small window at the very back of the truck and saw men lighting her home on fire. The place she grew up. The place she learned to walk, talk, read, and do magic, was slowly burning. Within moments, it turned into a pile of ash. Katrina felt tears form in the corner of her eyes. She bit her lip and held them back. Weakness could get her killed.

Shortly after she watched everything she cherished disappear, the truck found her aunt's home. They dragged Aunt Lisa out, torched the building, and threw her into the truck.

"You thought you'd get away from us?" said the guard. He wore a dark red suit and held a large shotgun in his arm.

Katrina looked at the guard's freshly blood stained hands. He was the one who shot her parents.

Aunt Lisa reached for Katrina's hand behind their backs. Their fingers locked. "Think of good things, not the bad," said Aunt Lisa.

"I didn't get to say goodbye," Katrina whispered. Then the tears began to fall. Katrina's heart ached. Her body slumped over.

Aunt Lisa squeezed Katrina's hand. "Then say it now." Aunt Lisa's heart ached too. The government had just killed her brother and his wife. Now, she was left to care for her niece. "Let's bless their souls," she whispered.

Katrina and Aunt Lisa closed their eyes and whispered a spell of good grace. They prayed for Katrina's parents then prayed for their own safety.

Aunt Lisa wore a weak smile. "Although our hearts are breaking, we must stay strong. We are witches and witches do not give up."

CHAPTER ONE

The truck door opened. "Get up and get out!" the guard yelled. The sun blinded them for a moment. They must have traveled for hours.

The camp looked horrid. A woman next to Katrina said they were at Ravensbrook. Katrina felt as if she had entered hell. She missed her parents, but she knew she could, she would survive.

Women and children were scattered all over the vast camp. Amongst them rested guards in dark clothing with rifles in their hands and whips behind them on their belts. Some had shades over their faces.

Katrina watched the faces of the prisoners. There was no laughter or joy anywhere. It was nothing like the town Katrina grew up in. Somehow, someway, she had to escape as soon as she could.

Katrina and her aunt were led through the center of the camp. Their hands still in handcuffs. Two women from the bus walk next to them. They were very quiet and never made eye contract. Most likely, they were fearful or just full of sadness. Knowing they were there for the same reason as Katrina, she wondered if one of them had heard their family die like she had.

People around the camp stopped their work and watched the new prisoners. The guards yelled and they quickly went back to work. Fear permeated the camp. It wasn't the kind of fear you put into a child to eat his vegetables. It was the fear of life or death. Of course, the prisoners all wanted desperately to live.

"Here!" yelled a guard. They were unhandcuffed. Two guards handed Katrina and the other new prisoners a bag of clothing along with other things with which to clean. They were given soap, a washcloth, and a toothbrush. "Strip!" ordered a guard.

Katrina looked around. It seemed everyone in the camp was looking at them. When she met their gaze, they looked down and walked away. "Here?" whispered Katrina.

"YES!" The guard pushed her on the ground. He grabbed his whip and snapped it onto her legs. Katrina felt a sting and burning. She fought back tears. *I will not show weakness. I will take what is dealt to me. I will not fight with the man who could take his gun to my head and kill me.*

Aunt Lisa fell to Katrina's side. "She is but a child. No need to be harsh." Aunt Lisa rubbed Katrina's legs then kissed Katrina's cheek. She whispered a soft poem into Katrina's ear, a poem in the native witch tongue she had often used. Katrina knew it meant love.

"You dare speak to me!" The guard raised his hand, ready to strike Aunt Lisa. His arm was grabbed by another man who appeared much stronger and taller. He seemed to come out of nowhere just in time to save them both from the pain of the whip.

"Stop taking the lack of coffee out on our new campers. Let them undress and move onto the next group. They will arrive shortly." The man who protected them walked away, without even looking at Katrina or her aunt. Katrina watched him walk away. She knew somehow, she had to find him and thank him for protecting her and her aunt. This man was not like the other guards. Even after being in the camp for a very short time, Katrina could see there was a difference. His energy and being was different. Katrina had to figure out why.

"STRIP!" the guard demanded. This time though, he put his whip back behind him and turned around to give them privacy.

It took them a second to take off the old dresses they wore and put on the grey burlap blouses and skirts. They were even given grey shoes, though Katrina's were much too small. She shoved her feet into them anyway.

Her aunt grabbed her hand and held it tightly. "We are dressed," she told the guard.

"Finally!" The guard walked around them. He looked them over, as if they were meat in a butcher shop. Then he faced the two and pointed to Aunt Lisa. "You will be a quilter." She was immediately grabbed and led away by two guards.

"Will I ever see her again?" Katrina asked.

"If you live to tomorrow. What kind of things can you do?"

"I can clean," she said. Her magic would help her clean. It was *magic* she did at home. She could certainly do it here.

"Fine you will clean. But, if your work is poor, you will be killed."

Katrina was grabbed and led away by two strong guards. Each one had their hands tightly wrapped around her thin arms.

They shoved her onto the floor of a dirty bathroom. It was gross and smelly and the worse thing Katrina had ever been around. There was vomit and all sorts of discharges on the floor and even the walls. It seemed the women preferred the ground and walls to the toilet. Katrina looked up and saw filth on the ceiling. She sat on the floor. Her world was crashing around her.

The other women in the bathroom area looked at her then ignored her. Katrina moved to the very corner of the bathroom and cried. She was alone. The feeling of being an orphan finally hit her just then. She began to sob.

The women quickly left the room afraid the crying would bring the guards in.

"I'd rather be alone," she whispered. She hugged her knees to her chest and felt the burlap fabric on her soft face. She sobbed even more.

As Katrina sobbed, she felt her witch powers burn within her. Normally, she would use her powers to solve her problems. She'd turn a bad day into a good day simply by casting a little spell. She'd make snowflakes fall perfectly or create a rainbow in the middle of the kitchen.

Her mother would laugh when she saw rainbows in the house.

"Katrina. I told you before, no rainbows," her mother would say. But, Katrina could hear softness in her voice. She knew her mother loved rainbows as much as Katrina did. Maybe even more, because she couldn't create them herself.

"Why do I have to be a witch?" Katrina remembered asking her father. She loved her powers most of the time, but there were times when she wanted to be normal. She didn't want to worry about the risk of someone finding out and her being killed simply because she was different.

She was young and wanted to have fun. She didn't want to have to learn how to control herself and her magic.

Her father would tell her, "Because the heavens above made you special, just like my sister and me." Then he would gently float up with the sweep of his arm.

She missed her mother's normalcy and her father's encouragement more than ever right then. But, the sound of her stomach rumbling reminded her that she was in her new home and had to do her best to blend in and not be killed because of her magic.

"I cast. I cast. I beg to thee above. Heavens, Hell and Land and Sea. Make me ignored. Make me no queen, so that I may blend into the world of the humans. Bless my mother and bless my father because I love them deeply." As Katrina whispered her spell, a soft light sparkled around the room then disappeared. She smiled for the first time since the death of her parents.

CHAPTER TWO

Katrina heard a sound at the door. It was the perfect time to test if the spell worked. A woman walked in and looked directly at her. Maybe the spell didn't work very well, Katrina thought. The woman lifted Katrina up by her arm.

"Why haven't you started cleaning this room yet?" asked the woman. She wore a cream-colored version of the same clothing Katrina wore. She looked important. And, she didn't look sad. Katrina had seen a lot of prisoners walking around the camp since she arrived at Ravensbrook. This one was different.

"I ... I didn't know where to start or what to use," Katrina said. She tried to shrink her body to make herself look small and weak.

The women shook her head and clicked her tongue against her teeth. "That making yourself look small won't work with me," the women said. "I'm Kelly. I monitor the maids at this camp."

Katrina nodded and looked up at the woman. The woman was large and older than her aunt. She had dark brown hair tied into a bun around her head. Her eyes were a bright blue, but bloodshot. She most likely cried every night wanting freedom, like they all did. Maybe Kelly prayed nightly for the Resistance to win. Her prayers had yet to be answered.

"If you want to stay alive here, you had better get to scrubbing." Kelly placed a bucket, soap, and a large sponge into Katrina's hand.

"Yes ma'am," Katrina said.

Kelly walked toward the door then turned back. "And you only have three hours to clean before Mr. Fog gets here to check on it. If he doesn't like it, he will shoot you."

Katrina felt a lump in her throat. Her body trembled. Kelly left and locked the door behind her. Katrina felt the tears weld up in her eyes, but there was no time for that now.

She had to clean and only had three hours to do it. The bathroom had 30 toilets, 20 showers, a large dressing room, and about 20 sinks to wash hands. There was only one way she could clean all that plus the ceiling, walls, and floor that quickly. She'd need her magic.

"Forgive me mother. I know you dislike magic combined with chores, but my fate now relies on this. I have no choice." Katrina looked up at the dark ceiling. She wished she could see her mother's face, instead of the filth.

She climbed onto one of the 10 benches in the middle of the large bathroom and held her hands.

"Take this bucket and fill it with water," she said. The bucket spun around and instantly water filled it to the brim. Soon two more buckets appeared, also filled with water. A glow swept around the room. Katrina felt her lips curl into a grin. There was a beauty in magic that she cherished.

"Take this sponge and make it multiply. One for each task and no more." The sponge grew into dozens, awaiting their command.

"Now, take the bubbles from the soap and fill the air. A clean bathroom is not clean if soap isn't used. Now, all of you clean," Katrina demanded.

The cleaning began. With one movement of her finger, buckets, sponges, and soapy bubbles flew around the room, cleaning everything and everywhere. Katrina watched, pointing here and there if she thought a little more cleaning was needed. Before she knew it, three hours passed. She heard the door unlock.

"Buckets, sponges, and soap, return to normal," whispered Katrina. The door slowly opened. Katrina stood there with just the bucket, sponge, and soap.

"Your name is?" the guard asked as he walked in with two other guards. They all looked around the room. One of the guards wiped here and there with a gloved finger. With each thing he checked, he placed his finger to his nose and smelled it.

"I'm Katrina," she said.

The guard testing the room looked over at her for the first time. "I'm Mr. Fog. You should fear me." He walked up to her and looked into her face. "You must put your hair back in a bun." He pointed to her long hair and removed the glove to touch a strand of it. It took all of Katrina's might not to throw him into the wall with a swing of her finger. "Each day, you must clean all the bathrooms in the camp."

"Yes. Sir," Katrina said.

"You will clean all seven bathrooms daily. The other six are like this one. If you don't do it, I will know and you will be punished or killed," said Mr. Fog. He leaned in closer to her. "And, if you thought the small whip this morning was punishment, you know nothing of the word."

The lump was back in Katrina's throat. Fear gripped her. She could only nod. This man was scary.

"Go find your sleeping tent. Then you can go to the mess hall to eat." Mr. Fog turned and walked out of the bathroom without another word. The other two guards followed him.

Katrina found herself relieved and even glad she was a witch at Camp Ravensbrook. Death would have been upon her if she had not used her powers to clean. "Thank you Father. Witchcraft is as good as you promised it would be."

CHAPTER THREE

Katrina left the bathroom and found her tent. She walked around and found the mess hall. It was massive and almost as dirty as the bathrooms. It seemed like there was no point in hunting for a clean area in the camp. There would never be a clean one, unless she was the one to clean it.

She saw a small line at the very back of the building and got onto it. She grabbed a small tray and a bowl from the side and moved along as the line moved. No one seemed to notice her. That made her feel safe. The spell worked. She was just like everyone else. She looked around the hall and spotty Aunt Lisa. Her heart leapt for joy.

"You're new here?" said the women serving food from behind a long table. There were dozens and dozens of children and mothers in the dining room area. Everyone had sad, burdened looks on their faces. Silence was *heard* throughout the room. Twelve guards with rifles in their hands and whips on their belts watched over the group. Katrina felt a chill run down her spine. This was now her life. She would have to get use to it.

"Yes. My aunt and I just got here this morning." Katrina pointed to her aunt sitting on a small bench toward the far end of the mess hall.

"Well, welcome." The woman placed a fake smile on her face. She took a large bowl and placed a large spoonful of chili in it. It looked like dirt and smelled like dog poop. Katrina took the bowl and nodded. The rest of the line continued along. Some of them looked like the walking dead.

The last stop on the food line was the corn bread station. It was a bright yellow, most likely from food coloring. It looked stale. She placed the small block onto her plate. Another gross item to eat, she thought.

Katrina was given a choice of orange juice or milk. "The orange tastes like medicine," the woman behind the station whispered. Katrina nodded, mouthed a quick thank you and grabbed the milk along with a fork, spoon, and a napkin. She couldn't deny her hunger. She longed for her mother's cooking, rather than the dirt on her plate.

Katrina remembered a time when her mother was stressed over something. She cooked the whole day, making dish after dish, just to keep herself busy. The house would smell as sweet as a bakery when Katrina returned home from school. It was amazing to walk in and see the pastries and food everywhere. It made her laugh and love her mother even more. Katrina wished she could cook like her mother.

"How many things did you bake today?" Katrina would ask when she walked in. She'd go into the kitchen expecting a mess, but her mother managed to keep everything neat and clean. Even when she made over a dozen bunt cakes, three or four different casseroles, and different soups. Everything was clean, not even a dish in the sink. And, her mother's apron always looked amazing.

"Oh not that many," her mother would reply because it was easier than actually counting. Normally, the number was in the teens.

The best part of her mother's stressful baking was that it fed the family and there was plenty left for her to prepare meals and treats for the Resistance group that lived in the tunnels at the edge of the city. They had little food and loved her cooking. It was a challenge for Katrina to go with her mother to the tunnels. But, her mother would hum the whole way and calm her down.

Katrina sorely missed the sounds of her mother's sweet humming. She missed the sweet smell of her baking and her giving soul. She believed her mother was inside of her, and would keep her safe.

Katrina took her plate and rushed to her aunt. "Auntie." She hugged Aunt Lisa. It made Katrina feel a bit hopeful and even a bit joyful to be with her aunt.

"Oh Katrina. I was so worried I wouldn't see you until it was time to sleep," said Aunt Lisa. Katrina still held her aunt tight.

A nearby guard came up and tapped her on the shoulder. He motioned for Katrina to sit down. "None of that here," he said. He turned and walked away.

Aunt Lisa nodded. Katrina waited until the guard moved away then stuck her tongue out. "This place sucks," she whispered to her aunt.

"It's better than death, Katrina. At least with magic we have hope." She moved closer to her niece. "We're in the same sleeping tent. I found a good place to sleep. The women who make quilts invited us to sleep in their section with them. It's cleaner than the rest of the tent. Many of the grandmothers are in that section, so it's not too loud. There are only a few children."

Katrina nodded. She took the spoon and tasted the chili. It tasted as disgusting as it looked. She spit it out. Aunt Lisa laughed. The guard from before cleared his throat instead of walking over.

"You forgot the spell?" Aunt Lisa poked out her tongue and twisted it. She quietly sang to herself then stopped. Katrina nodded and did the same thing.

The spell turned a basic dish into whatever she wanted it to be. So, while the others were eating the worst chili ever, Katrina enjoyed a bowl of her favorite cereal and milk. Her aunt was enjoying freshly made pasta with meatballs. And, they could do this for the rest of their time in the camp. The camp would still be hell, but at least Katrina and her aunt could enjoy meals they loved. It was the best they could do, at least for the time being.

CHAPTER FOUR

Katrina looked around the mess hall as she ate. She admired the women and children who walked around to keep active. Some were trying hard to appear happy. Most just sat and ate their meal. In the very corner sat Kelly, eating some carrots and a bowl of a white soup. It didn't seem fair. Why did she get different food? Wasn't she a prisoner also?

The moment Aunt Lisa and Katrina got up from the

table, a guard instructed them, "Go back to work." They made sure not to finish their meals, even though they could have. It would look suspicious if someone actually ate all the disgusting food on the plate.

Outside the hall, Aunt Lisa gave Katrina a quick pat on the back. "I'll see you tonight." Then she walked away.

"Shine shoes." A man walked toward Katrina with a bucket and a scrubbing brush. She sat on a small chair in the middle of the campground and waited for the first guard to come. Soon there was a line of men waiting for her to shine their shoes. She couldn't help but smile when she saw the cleaning set that looked a lot like something she'd be given by her father. Instead of a lemonade stand like most little girls do in the city. Her father taught her to use magic to make the task of shoe shining easier and fun. Katrina would sing a song to herself, a soft spell to make the polish even better. Katrina remembered sitting outside the big business building with a small umbrella, a stool, and enough supplies to shine a few dozen shoes. The moment they saw her cute pigtails and sweet face, men and women would stop and have her shine their shoes before they walked inside the building.

Katrina remembered one day a man who carried a cup of coffee and dozens of papers, stopped by her stand. He saw Katrina had no one waiting for a shine. It seemed to make him sad. He placed his papers and coffee on the floor and called his boss to say he would be late. He was getting his shoes shined by the little girl on the sidewalk. It didn't take long for a dozen or so people from his office to come out just to help her out too.

Although shoe shining at Camp Ravensbrook was different, she sang the soft song. "Oh grumpy be happy. Oh grumpy be happy. Smile. Smile. Smile.

Shine bright. Shine bright. Happy. Happy. Happy." It was such a silly song, but it brought a smile to her face and reminded her of a time when there was no Resistance. A time when there was nothing to worry about.

Before the war, life was good. There was a happy harmony around the world. There were no wars. There was no violence. People didn't fight. Then, a new ruler took over Germany. He decided to kill the Queen of England. He wanted to take control of the whole world in under a year. That's when the world changed. Witches were then considered demons and killed because they were different and could do things others could not. The Nazis military took over. If you weren't a member, you were considered part of the Resistance. People were killed because of this. Families would hide in the forest, in attics, or other areas to avoid the Nazis military. Those who were found were put into camps, if they weren't killed.

Her father joined the Resistance the moment his best friend was killed. He couldn't stand by any longer and not fight. Her father became an important member of the Resistance. He was a powerful warlock and knew ways to win. He knew what was to come. He had planned fighting the military long before it even came about. Now, that plan was gone, along with the home she grew up in.

Katrina loved the memories of her father working hard to protect her future. She could smile and sing the song as she shined each shoe for the guards, who had guns and whips ready to hurt her if she did something wrong.

"Hi," said a man who walked up to her and sat down. "I see you've gotten settled since this morning." Katrina looked up and admired the man in front of her. He had a strong face and gentle eyes. He didn't look like the other guards. His soul was clear of evil thoughts. It was easy to see he didn't want to hurt people. He smiled at Katrina and didn't get mad when she smiled back.

"You were the one who stopped the man from whipping me and my aunt," Katrina whispered.

"That I was." He leaned back into the small chair. "I think that earns me a nice shoe shine," he said.

Katrina had been shining shoes for hours. The sun began to set. The prisoners slowly walked to their tents to sleep. Katrina worked hard to shine his very dirty boots.

"Thank you for taking sure care with my boots," he said.

Katrina tried hard not to smile. Without him, she might have been whipped and badly hurt. Or worse, her aunt could have been hurt.

"What's your name?" he asked. He watched her closely as she shined his boots.

"Katrina," she said. She hummed as she shined and buffed.

"I'm Peter. You're very pretty. How did you come to be here?"

Her body shivered at his compliment. She had never been called pretty before. "My father and mother were killed yesterday. Our house was burned down, too. My aunt and I were brought here. My parents were part of the Resistance."

He observed Katrina carefully. "I see. What do you think of this war and our ruler?"

"You want to know my honest thoughts?" She looked up at him. "Or, will you kill me if I'm honest?" He didn't look like a man who would hurt her, but then not all the guards looked evil.

Peter laughed. "I have no intention of killing you or letting anyone else kill a pretty young girl like yourself.

Trust me, you can be honest."

"I hate this war and agree with the Resistance," she said as she continued shining his shoes.

"If I had a choice, I'd be working for the other side." Peter lowered his eyes. "But the health of my family is the most important thing to me. Plus, my uncle hired me to work here."

"I respect that choice." She smiled at him. They both felt a spark as they stared at each other for those few seconds.

"There's something special about you." Peter moved a little closer. Katrina instantly looked down. The burn of curiosity filled her body, but she tried hard to focus on the boot she was buffing.

Peter reached out and softly took hold of her chin. Then he placed his lips upon hers. The electric sense of passion was something neither of them expected. His tongue slid into her mouth. He closed his eyes and melted into the kiss, savoring the feeling.

"Wow," Katrina whispered when he parted his lips from hers.

"You'll be mine forever." Peter got up from the chair and started to walk away. "Thanks for the shoeshine. I intend to come back for seconds soon."

Katrina traced her lips with her finger. She licked them and could still taste the light flavor of mint over them. Peter had just changed her outlook on the place she thought would be her hell. Maybe Peter could make this a much better form of hell.

CHAPTER FIVE

Peter breathed in the night air and looked around. No one had seen what just happened. He smiled to himself and ran his fingers over his lips. "I could get used to those lips." He walked to the guards' quarters on the other side of the camp. It was a long walk and gave him plenty of time to think about the kiss.

There was something about Katrina that was unlike any other girl in the camp. She didn't fear him. She wasn't ready to defend herself. Instead, Katrina was soft and petite. Her long black hair hugged her face and covered her from the eyes of others. Her small body made her seem weak, but Peter knew she was stronger than most of the girls in Ravensbrook. The soft freckles on her rosy cheeks begged to be touched by his strong hands. There was something that drew him to her. From the way she spoke to the way she walked.

He stopped a whip for her the moment she got off the bus. That was unlike him and yet he did it. "I have to control this urge," he whispered to himself as he walked closer to the guards' quarters. The loud laughter and poker chips hitting the table could be heard from outside. Peter took a deep breath and walked inside.

"Hey Peter!" Captain Henry yelled from the poker table. Six guards sat at the table with Captain Henry. There were forty or fifty other guards standing around. Their job for the night was over. Only a dozen armed guards watched over the camp late at night. The guards' quarters was massive and held them all easily. Each guard had his own bed and could do whatever he wanted when off duty. They had permission from the captain himself. Captain Henry was Peter's uncle. He let Peter get away with a number of things. It was awesome for Peter.

"Hey guys," said Peter. He spoke, but his mind was still on Katrina. He quickly found his bed and began to remove his boots. He felt tired, but knew it would be hard to sleep. He had to remove the thoughts of Katrina from his mind as quickly as possible. He inspected his boots carefully and couldn't find any spots of dirt. She did an amazing job.

"Did you see that new girl?" A guard named Josh yelled from the corner of the room.

"Wasn't she hot?" another guard said from the poker table.

They were talking about Katrina. There went his goal of going to sleep. "Yeah. Her name is Katrina," Peter said. For some reason jealousy was sneaking up on him and he was having a hard time controlling it.

"I'd say she's definitely worthy of some midnight fun," Josh said.

Everyone knew what he was talking about. The thought of Katrina being used by these jerks made Peter clench his fist. He held back the urge to punch his friend in the nose. Instead, he thought about what to say.

He looked down and continued to remove his boots. They still looked great, even after walking to the quarters. Something about that girl ... she made everything effortless and somehow did a great job at it as well. "She sleeps in the quilters' quarters with her aunt. So, it's out of the question." Peter removed his hat. His long shaggy hair stuck to the inside of it. Some of the guards laughed. They knew the quilters were off limits to everyone. The older women didn't need to be harmed. It was pointless to bother them.

"Oh dang!" said Josh. I might have to get creative with that sexy little girl." All the guards agreed.

"Don't count on it. I'm thinking of making her mine before you can." Peter laughed. If he claimed her at least the others would leave her alone. And, he would treat her much better than those jerks would. He liked Katrina and didn't want to see her get hurt. He just wanted to get to know her and kiss her as many times as he could. He wanted her and would do anything he could to have her.

"Finally, Peter is coming out of his shell and is going to take a hot little chick as his own!" Captain Henry said. "You all have been ordered to leave Katrina for Peter. Have your pick of the other girls, but she is his."

"Thank you Captain." Peter nodded and smiled. He sat down to play a game of poker before it was finally time to go to bed. He got a flush and even a straight while playing the game. He was on a roll. The other players teased him for making Katrina his sudden good luck charm, even when she wasn't there.

In the morning, he would be able to start the courting of Katrina and truly make her his own. And, thanks to the captain, he didn't have to worry about the competition, or worse, someone taking advantage of the girl he really liked.

CHAPTER SIX

Katrina woke to some of the others in her tent looking at her. It seemed like her spell suddenly stopped working. This didn't happen often. It freaked her out. She did her best to avoid people the rest of the day. And, fortunately, Kelly hadn't been looking for her either. Katrina felt very lucky.

"There is a guard looking for you," a young girl told Katrina. The girl found Katrina hiding in the corner of the laundry room. Her legs close to her body, hugging herself just like she had done the first day in the camp.

The laundry room was cleaner and smelled much nicer than the bathrooms. Plus, being in the corner behind all the clothing stopped anyone from seeing her. Katrina had seen Peter asking around for her and raced in the room to hide. She had been there for an hour or so.

The girl moved closer. "At least I think it's you. You're Katrina right?" she asked this time. A smile fell across her thin face.

Katrina nodded and hugged herself even more. "I noticed. I don't want to be found by him."

"Is he really that bad?" asked the girl.

Katrina didn't understand why she was afraid. Peter wasn't bad. He was nice and kind. How could he be bad? "I don't know. He kissed me the other night."

"And that's all? Lucky you." The young girl laughed as she folded the clothing and bedding. "I've been raped five or six times since coming here. It didn't stop until I was claimed by Captain Henry. The guards left me alone for a while. Then the captain got tired of me."

"Raped?" Katrina's mind tumbled and turned. She hadn't thought about that before. Rape was in this camp. She nearly cried for the young girl before her. The girl was a couple of years younger than herself. She had been forced into a hell no one deserved.

"The guard looking for you has never done that to any girl here. In fact, he has stopped other guards from hurting girls." The young girl picked up the laundry baskets. As she walked away, she said, "You should be happy that he just kissed you and wants to protect you and not hurt you. This place is hell if you don't have a guard on your side."

"He wants to protect me." Katrina whispered to herself. She remembered how her aunt said to look for the good inside of people. And, now it was her time to find it.

"Hey guys." Peter walked into the laundry room. "Have you seen a girl named Katrina?" He was asking for her by name. Katrina pulled her legs to her body even closer and tried to be as quiet as possible.

"Oh, I heard you have claimed her?" said a guard who followed Peter in. "Good job, man. Finally, you get to enjoy the action here."

Peter laughed it off. "If you see her, send her my way." He quickly walked away.

Katrina had been claimed. What did that even mean? And, why was that guard and the young girl saying the same thing? She had to go find her aunt and ask her what it meant and if it was a good thing.

"Auntie." Katrina raced into the quilting tent.

Aunt Lisa looked up from her work. "Yes Katrina." She looked weak and tired. Her fingers were covered with dots of blood from the poor quality needles she had to quilt with. Quilting was once a passion of her aunt's. Camp Ravensbrook turned it into a chore and made it painful. But, still, it was better for her aunt to sew, than do more manual things, so she didn't complain.

"Can we talk?" Katrina nodded a Hello to the other ladies.

"Yes." Her aunt got up from the quilting square and walked outside with her. She put her hand on Katrina's shoulder. "Is something wrong?"

"A guard wants to claim me," Katrina said, getting right to the point.

"I heard," said Aunt Lisa. "His name is Peter right? He was the one who stopped the whip from hitting us when we arrived." She placed her quilting needle into the top of her hair. A small smile crept over her face. "I feel he is a good man. A strong man. A man who can fill your soul with love. And, he can also bring us to safety."

"But . . ." The words her aunt spoke were crazy. How could she know all these things?

Aunt Lisa lifted Katrina's face up. She looked into her eyes. "He's not the type of man who will rape a woman. He's a lover. He's the man who kissed you last night and told the other guards to leave you alone."

"What about what we are?" Katrina said. The glow of her magic soul could be seen for miles, if someone looked hard enough. And, she felt that if Peter was that someone to look, she would be dead before she could cast a spell.

"He isn't like the others. He's ... yours," whispered Aunt Lisa. "Go to him and be his love. He is our path to the Resistance." She turned and went back to her quilting without saying another word.

Katrina watched as the smartest person she ever

knew walked away and went back to the chore she had been given. Katrina tried to swallow the words she just heard. "How can he be my love? He's a guard? And worse, he's a mortal."

Her mother often said she cherished the love she and her father had, but it was hard for her to be placed into a home of witches when she wasn't one herself. Her father made sure his wife was given the respect she deserved. He felt comforted to know theirs was a true love. A love that Katrina wanted more than anything. Could Peter be that love?

Peter found Katrina walking toward the mess hall. "Why haven't you come to see me?" he whispered in her ear from behind. He took her hand into his and walked her to a corner of the camp where no one could see them. "I've been hunting for you all morning." The smile on his face was brighter than the sun.

Katrina looked up at him. She felt the flutter of passion in her body. "Because that kiss was a mistake." She looked down. She tried to relax her tensed body.

"You didn't like the feel of my lips on yours?"

"I did." Katrina hung her head slightly to hide the blush rising in her face. "It's against the rules."

"Sweetheart, I'm a guard. I make the rules." He pulled her close to him, so close she was unable to get free. She quickly melted into his strong arms. "And, right now I have a rule that you will be mine." He tried to place his lips on hers once again, but she pulled away. She was afraid she wouldn't be able to withstand being consumed with pleasure.

"I heard you talking to the guards about how I'm yours," Katrina said.

"Would you rather me let you be alone and not save you from those horny jerks who care nothing about women?" Peter stood back and folded his arms. "You've heard right? The girls get raped here and no one cares about their cries. No one will save you if it's not me."

"But, I fight for freedom," she whispered.

"And, I respect that. Maybe someday I'll join you in that fight." Peter bent down and looked into her eyes. "For now, I simply want to cherish the time I have with you. I don't know how much longer that may be. To me, you are more than just a girl. I want to make you mine so I can keep you safe." He closed his eyes and moved forward to kiss her again.

"Wait." she said, stopping him for the second time.

"Yeah?" Peter tried hard to hide his annoyance.

"You'll keep my aunt safe as well?" Katrina said.

"Yes. Of course. Whoever you want me to keep safe. I will," Peter said. "Now can I kiss you, please?"

Katrina stood on her tiptoes and placed her lips onto his. She kissed him this time. His arms wrapped around her and held her tightly as they melted into each other and kissed deeply. It was the first time in the last few days that she was actually happy.

CHAPTER SEVEN

That night, Katrina heard the soft screams of girls. It was when she was about to fall asleep that the noises started. It wasn't until the little girl in the laundry room told Katrina about the things that happened at night that she began to notice and listen.

The sounds weren't nearby and it seemed the others in her tent slept through them. Sure, some of them cried in their sleep, praying for freedom, but screams from those girls didn't keep them awake. "I have to see what's going on," said Katrina. Fear was on the back burner as she hopped out of the uncomfortable bed. She tiptoed out of the tent. She peeked around the courtyard. She became alert when she noticed a few guards walking around half asleep. They held their flashlights, but didn't seem to notice her. It was the first time she was thankful for the dull lifeless outfit that blended into the fabric of the tents.

Katrina raced toward the crying and screams. As she got closer, the screams grew louder. Everyone nearby could hear it, but no one did anything to stop it or investigate. She wondered why.

"What are they doing?" Katrina whispered to herself. Were girls being raped or could they be killing the Jews? Were they making them break rocks or bricks at this time? No. Katrina had not seen any Jews in the camp yet and most of the guards were in their quarters already.

Katrina snuck to the doorway of the tent where the screams were coming from. The tent was sectioned off and had doors to different areas. She silently crept along until she ran down a hallway with her was outside the door where the screams were coming from. Her heart raced. She wondered if she should turn around and go back. Katrina stood at the door. She slowly opened it.

Katrina immediately regretted opening it. Inside were five beds and a girl laid on top of each. Guards stood in a circle around the beds. Several other guards were on top of the girls.

There in the corner, she saw the young girl from the

laundry room. She was on a corner bed with a much older, heavier man on top of her. His hand covered her mouth so that she couldn't scream in his ears. Two other guards held down her hands so she couldn't scratch or push the man off. Tears slid down her face.

The other girls struggled and wept, and cried out for mercy. Katrina watched in horror. A wave of disgust flooded her. She quickly thought of a spell of relief.

Luckily for her, the guards were too distracted to notice her standing at the edge of the doorway. Then she heard her mother's voice. "No stranger may touch you. If they do, turn them into frogs and bring me their legs so we can eat them for dinner."

Turn them into frogs. Katrina could do that in a second, but then the others guards would know of her powers and most likely the girls would tell others. She'd be killed. But, she had to do something. She had to stop the pain. This was rape and it was terribly wrong. No one should suffer like this. "We already suffer hell in the camp, we should at least be able to sleep in peace," she whispered.

Katrina knew it was time to take action. She made a black cloud cover her. Taking the power from her inner body, she made sure no one would see her while she worked to save these girls. Her fist shook as her power rushed into her body.

She waved her hands into the air and guards flew into the wall as she fired as many spells as she could. She didn't kill anyone, but she did cause them to suffer, just like they made the girls suffer.

The guards jumped off the girls. They raced around the room to find out what was causing this attack. Katrina aimed her spells at their legs, causing them to fall to the ground in pain. The girls ran from the room. Then Katrina gave the guards a sickness unlike any other. From uncontrollable diarrhea, to throwing up blood, to hives all over their body.

With every magic spell, the sounds turned from women crying to men crying. Katrina turned and walked away. She smiled. It was the first time she had ever used her real powers to help someone. Often, she'd cast small spells, but this time the magic came from her body and her mind. She felt exhilarated. It was a feeling that had been burning in her body since she was born. It made her wonder if this was the reason she was at Camp Ravensbrook. Was she placed in this camp to help the prisoners? And, could she do it alone?

Katrina found her way back to her tent. She snuggled into bed, next to her aunt's bed. "Let the men never heal," she barely whispered. She didn't want those men to feel well enough to try again. She wanted them to suffer.

CHAPTER EIGHT

The next morning, a woman in high heels walked through the camp. She wore an all-white jumpsuit and had red hair tied in a tight bun on the very top of her head. She wore too much make up and smelled liked she bathed in expensive, bad smelling perfume. This woman was scary. The guards stopped chatting when they saw her walking closer to them. Her name was Iona Brooke. She was the original owner of Camp Ravensbrook and everyone called her Lion. It was told that she would stalk her prey from behind and kill them before they could defend themselves.

Lion tried to look nice and tried to appear kind. She would smile and laugh to make the guards relax. But, the moment they let their guard down, she would take the whip from her belt and bring them to their knees. She had no problem whipping a man, a woman, or even the youngest child in the camp. She was an evil woman.

The strangest thing about Lion was that she was nice to the quilters. She would walk into the quilting tent and greet all the quilters. She'd check on their progress with the dozens of quilts they were making. Sometimes, she'd even bring them glasses of ice water. The women appreciated her for this. And, it kept them on their best behavior.

Lion had a dark evil plan. She rented her land to the Nazis party so they could turn it into a camp for women and children camp. She did this as soon as the war began in 1941. Along with payment, Lion requested the new owners give her the right to visit the camp whenever she wanted. General Mark, who ran the camp, had been hesitant about agreeing to that demand, but finally agreed.

Lion's plan was to take her camp back soon. She had been stealing supplies and money from the military. Once she took the camp back, she would kill everyone in it. This would make her the most powerful woman with the Nazis party. They'd have to realize her power.

Peter ignored Katrina that day. "Why are you avoiding me?" she whispered to him as he stood by the doorway to the mess hall. He was guarding the entrance, pushing prisoners inside. "Why are you being so mean?"

"Quiet. I'll explain later," Peter whispered as soft as he could.

Katrina knew their relationship was a secret. She didn't want either of them to be killed because of the passion and respect they had for each other. She knew they had to be very careful. Although Peter brightened her life, she knew the camp was dangerous and had an evil hatred for it.

Lion walked into the mess hall shortly after Katrina and her aunt sat down to eat their food. Her high heels clicked loudly on the ground floor. Everyone stopped eating and watched Lion. It seemed like some even stopped breathing. She walked slowly.

Lion began her inspection by looking over Peter. She checked his gun that rested on his hip and she checked to make sure his posture was just right. Katrina could see the sweat on Peter's forehead, even from a distance. Now, she understood why they couldn't speak.

Katrina sat and watched as Lion roamed around. She took her time tasting every dish. She walked past every table and took her time choosing three prisoners who were then taken to a secret place. All the prisoners knew there were four things that happened at Camp Ravensbrook, they were punished, did chores, lived, or died. There was nothing else. One of the prisoners taken was the young girl she spoke with in the laundry room and helped the night before.

Katrina walked out of the mess hall with other women. Tears made their way into Katrina's eyes. The young girl couldn't have been more than 12 or 13 years old and there she was, dragged from her family. The Nazis party were to blame for this war and hatred, but Lion was to blame for this current act of inhumanity.

They watched as Lion followed the three prisoners. The girls' families cried. Other prisoners tried to calm their fears and sooth their souls. Of course, there was no way to soothe the pain. Then they heard the three gunshots. Katrina wept and shook. What if she had helped them? Should she have? Or, was it a lost cause?

Katrina tried to change her thoughts. She didn't want to remember the three gunshots and knew the young girls were being tossed into the pile of dead bodies that rested in the grass on the outer side of the camp. She closed her eyes and remembered her mother. She remembered a time when her mother was getting all dressed up for a ball in her honor. It was before the Resistance. It was before Hitler became ruler of Germany, before he began killing the Jews and taking prisoners. It was a time when people laughed and enjoyed each other. Fearing for their lives from a crazed dictator wasn't a thought.

Katrina's mother sat on the chair and did her makeup. Katrina watched in wonder, wishing she could put on the fake eyelashes or brush her cheeks with a soft pink colored powder. "Mother, why can't I wear makeup too?" Katrina already knew the answer though, she was too young. She was only eleven years old and much too young to experience men looking at her because of the makeup she wore.

Her mother smiled into the mirror then turned and looked at Katrina. "I wear make up to make myself look prettier and hide the wrinkles on my face." She pointed to her eyes and forehead. "You, my lovely, are too beautiful to ever need such things on your face."

That made Katrina smile. She breathed in deeply and helped her mother tie the perfect bun on top of her head. She then helped her mother find the perfect dancing shoes for the ball.

Katrina opened her eyes. The other prisoners began calming down. They went back into the mess hall and continued eating. This was life in the camp. Lion roamed the camp. She looked for anyone who would cross her, so she could teach them a lesson. Thankfully, Lion left late that night. Before she left though, she had she killed over twenty women and children for no reason at all. The first three were those three girls taken from the mess hall.

That night cries of anguish filled the camp. It was hard to sleep. The guards didn't do anything about the screams. They didn't roam the camp, hunting for girls they could claim. Instead, the guards played poker. They walked the grounds and stood their post. They tried to forget Lion's visit. Katrina closed her eyes and tried to sleep. These horrors were too difficult to comprehend. Her aunt reached across the bed and held her hand. "It's okay, Katrina, my sweet." She began to sing the same song her mother sang to her when she was young. It brought tears to her eyes and hope to her soul.

CHAPTER NINE

Peter and the other guards felt relief that Lion didn't come after them this time. Only weeks ago, Lion had come to the camp and put all the guards on notice. She took aim at many of them, including Peter. He lost a friend who stood right next to him, simply because the man didn't salute her quickly enough.

She was truly evil. During the war, women were considered insignificant. But, Lion was feared. She took pride in that. She enjoyed it.

"That bitch is crazy," said one of the guards in the quarters. Although Lion was gone, tension and death lingered over the camp.

"I don't know why she felt like she had to kill those prisoners. They didn't even do anything wrong," said a guard who was new to the camp. He had been working at a grain mill only miles away. After the Resistance burned it down, he was transferred to Camp Ravensbrook. He didn't seem to fit into their group very well, but he was trying.

The guards sat in their quarters eating danishes and drinking expensive beer that Lion had left behind as a thank you for doing a good job. This time they were given gifts instead of death.

"At least she didn't kill one of us," Josh said. He lit a cigarette and tried to relax, but his finger twitched. "I can't stand that woman." He took a long, slow drag.

Peter sat in the corner with his legs up on a footstool. He listened to the radio playing and tried to enjoy the soft music Hitler had approved for them. He was sad, but also happy that he had Katrina. He feared though that Katrina would be killed if Lion knew about the passion they had for each other. Thankfully, Lion didn't learn of their romance. Neither Katrina nor her aunt were harmed.

He felt bad for having to ignore Katrina, but she understood after seeing Lion walk into the mess hall and heard the shots that killed those prisoners. Lion made Peter hate his job, but because his uncle worked there, he had no choice but to follow his command. When the time was right, he would choose to side with the Resistance.

"You're pretty quiet over there, Peter," Josh said.

"Just thinking and listening to the music." Peter faked a smile. All together, twenty women and children were killed that afternoon. With each death, a pain flooded his soul. But, he had to hold his head high. He had no choice. None of the guards were killed, but some were whipped for talking back to Lion. Still, Peter was very thankful that he wasn't one of them.

"The girls get a break tonight," announced Captain Henry.

"Yeah. Some of my girls lost their mothers or some kind of family," said a guard lying on his bed. His name was Tim. He often had three or four girls nightly. "I don't want to deal with no crying chick while she's trying to do her chore." He laughed.

Peter shook his head. If he could go to Katrina and hug away her tears, he would. He just knew she was crying right then. He knew she was friendly with the young girl killed earlier. Katrina would be heartbroken never to speak to her again. Sadly, hugging was not something normal within the camp. Rape was normal. Death was normal. He hated it with an extreme disgust.

"Peter, I heard you claimed that Katrina girl," Tim said.

"Yeah. So what?"

"Is she any good? I know she's good at cleaning a bathroom, but is that all?"

Peter didn't know what to say. If he said too much, Tim might want to test her out. He thought for a moment. "She's as good as any girl. She still weeps and tries to kick me off." Neither was true. "But she takes it and will continue to take it." The words stung as they left his mouth. The guards around him cheered. They were glad he was finally getting into the swing of being a guard.

But the truth was, Peter knew Katrina wouldn't mind being with him. He could picture her holding him tight and whispering sweet things into his ears. She would allow him to take her virgin body and make it his own. He could feel her passion with each shy kiss they shared between chores. When they kissed, they melted into one another. He promised her the world with every ounce of energy he could give her. He promised to free her. He promised to love and cherish her, until her last breath. Katrina loved him and he loved her. There was a passion within her eyes when they kissed. It would not be raped, it would be love making. And, if he could marry her, he would.

"Good. I'm glad you've finally picked a girl to play with," the captain said. "Let's play some cards, boys." The night continued with a game of poker and chatting about the news of the war and Hitler's plans to kill as many Jews as possible.

CHAPTER TEN

The next day there was a quiet sadness over the camp. The silence was painful to experience. Katrina sat in the mess hall, using her magic to turn the disgusting oatmeal she was eating into a plate of eggs, with bacon and a hash brown. She sat with her aunt, who still had tears in her eyes.

"We have to be careful," Aunt Lisa whispered. "I don't want you to be next."

"I have Peter on my side," Katrina said.

"He's just a guard and has no rank in this hellish place. You must use your magic to protect yourself and free yourself when the time is right." Before Katrina could reply with a question, Aunt Lisa got up and went to the quilting room. Katrina went to do her chores.

"We have a new shipment coming in today." Tim walked past the bathrooms. "About 50 worthless Jews. We have to take them to the chamber. With luck, they will die quickly." Katrina's breath stopped. Why did they have to do such things? Couldn't they have the Jewish people do chores and help around the camp? With twenty women and children killed the day before, additional workers were needed in all areas.

The bus arrived shortly after she heard the guards speak. It was a dirty old bus that was packed full of people of all ages and sizes. Katrina watched from the bathroom. She eyed the Jewish people that, for some reason, Hitler hated. Hitler wanted them gone. He wanted nothing more than to rid Germany of a people he didn't know anything about.

Then Katrina saw Alice. She walked off the bus with her hands intertwined. Her mother wasn't there. Alice most likely was alone. Her mother and father were probably killed because they were Jewish. "Oh no," Katrina whispered to herself. "Not her too."

Katrina recognized her from her old neighborhood. Alice was a witch too. But, she was also Jewish. Her father was part of the Resistance. Katrina closed her eyes. "Meet me as soon as you can," she thought to Alice.

"But, I will be killed shortly," Alice thought back. "There is nothing I can do. May the Resistance win." She turned away from sight.

Katrina wouldn't take that. She wouldn't allow these horrible people to kill Alice. Katrina began to run as fast as she could toward the bus. "Light and Light wake them up. With twenty less, we need help. Take my soul and fill it with courage. Mother. Father. I need you now." She ran with all her might. She was chanting the spell over and over until she found herself in front of the strongest guard and biggest guard she had seen yet. He was pulling the Jewish prisoners by the chains around their necks.

"Please sir, I could use her help," Katrina said. She pointed to Alice. "We all could use their help."

"Her help with what?" another guard said with a smug grin across his ugly mean face. Katrina bit her lip to stop herself from turning him into the slug he should be. She could have done it to every guard in this hellish place with a single spell, but she didn't.

"We lost twenty workers yesterday and need the help to finish our chores," Katrina said. "She and I would be a great team when it comes to maid service. I'll be twice as fast and twice as good." Her mind wandered into his mind and she took control of him and the other guards. It took all her power to make him nod and agree.

"Fine. These disgusting Jews can live. But if they don't work hard enough, harder than every prisoner in this place, they will be killed one by one." The guard pointed his long finger into her face.

"Yes sir." Katrina bowed. "I promise, we will teach them well." One by one, the guards let them free and other prisoners came to their aid to show them the way to their quarters and to begin to clean and keep the camp in order.

"Thank you," Alice said as they walked arm in arm toward the bathroom. "I thought I was dead."

"We're not alive yet," Katrina said. "Our powers can only do so much without being noticed and killed for it."

"They killed twenty people yesterday?" Alice asked.

Katrina nodded and hung her head low. "The woman they call Lion came to this camp and just kept shooting people for no reason. Mothers lost children. Children lost mothers. Children lost siblings, for no reason at all." Katrina held back her tears. "My aunt and I are blessed to still be here."

"This place is hell. No one should be here," Alice said clasping Katrina's arm tight.

"True." Katrina tried to smile. "But it's better than being dead and thrown into a corner. It's very easy for them to kill us all."

Alice nodded. "My father and mother were killed. I ran, but someone told them about me. They found me and I was taken."

"My aunt is all I have left," Katrina said.

"Then we have to stick together and live through this hell, until we have a plan to get out and stay out," Alice said. Her brave words were something Katrina needed to hear more than ever right then. Alice was brave and full of heart, while at times, Katrina was weak and shy. They were the perfect team to run from Camp Ravensbrook.

"Welcome to the home you hope to leave." Katrina laughed. She took Alice around to explore and find out where things were. Then the chores began for the day. With magic powers and two witches, the cleaning of all seven bathrooms would take half the time and half the effort. That would please the stupid ugly guard who let the Jews be workers rather than kill them.

CHAPTER ELEVEN

The girls began to get ready for their chore. As she prepared, Katrina remembered a time when Alice and her were best friends, until Katrina's family moved to be closer to the Resistance.

"Let's play on the ceiling." They would float into the air so their feet could walk on the ceiling. Their parents would get upset when they walked into the room and saw chalk and glue all over the ceiling. It was a fun memory. It was even more fun than flying while their mothers tried to bathe them together.

Katrina remembered a time when they started school in the city. She remembered just how hard it was for them to relax and not use their gifts. After being schooled at home and then in a magic school miles away, it was hard not to use powers daily. But, somehow they managed to do it.

"We're moving to the city," she told Alice one day. Tears flooded Alice's face. The two best friends were about to part ways. It seemed though that fate stepped in and brought her friend back to her in her time of need. Katrina was actually happy.

"So we're maids?" Alice said.

"Yes, we are." Katrina prepared the buckets and sponges. She took her time so that she and Alice could talk and catch up. And, before they were around other people.

"This cleaning stuff sounds gross," Alice said making a face.

"Actually, with our gift of cleaning, it's as quick as a snap of a finger," Katrina said. Alice nodded and finally understood. With magic, the act of cleaning seven gross bathrooms every single day was not as hard as it would be for someone else. Maids they were, but they were magical maids.

"I see," said Alice. "What does your aunt do here?" Then she realized Katrina's aunt might have been killed. "I'm sorry..." She trailed off and hung her head down.

"No. It's okay. She's one of the quilters."

"Thank the stars," Alice said. She placed her fingers

on her neck.

"Did you?" Katrina pointed at Alice's neck.

"It's all I have left." Alice pulled down her shirt just enough to show the Star of David resting on the very top of her collarbone. "My grandmother gave it to my mother and she gave it to me." Tears welded up in Alice's eyes. "I can't let the Nazis guards take this."

Katrina leaned forward and wrapped her arms around her weeping friend. She tried to ease her pain. But, of course it wasn't something that could be done. Death of a family member was something no one could overcome in such a short time, if at all. Katrina tried her best. "I feel your pain too," she whispered.

"As much as I hate this place, I'm glad you are here with me." Alice pulled herself free, tucking the star back under her shirt. She wiped her eyes free of tears.

Katrina looked over the bathroom. The sounds of the shots from the day before still rang in her ears. "This place is hell, but with each other and our gifts, we can do things to help these women and children."

Katrina's father had taught her that helping was the way the Land of Witches freed themselves from the devil and evil witches who aimed to kill instead of cherish the earth they lived on. With Alice by her side, Katrina felt she could help. She could share her gift and remove the pain of the people here, if only for a moment. She could lessen the hatred of this place. She could calm the tears at night. She could remove the nightly rapes and the screams that came from it. With Alice, she would be able to do more.

"We have to be careful," Alice said. "I want to help as much as you do. But, I'm a Jew. If I'm caught, there is no hope for me holding onto my life. I'd be killed the moment I'm accused." Shivers ran down her spine. "But, I know I must fight for the Resistance. We must."

"Little by little we will," Katrina said. "But, first we must command these mops to clean the bathrooms." She locked arms with Alice and they walked around the bathroom. The smell was so bad, just from the day before. It was the first of their cleaning and the start of their plan to better the hell within this camp as best they could.

"Is this the new girl?" Kelly, the head maid, walked in without warning, just as Katrina was about to cast the cleaning spell. "You're a Jew right?" Kelly look angry.

Alice nodded and bowed.

"Then you better do a great job, or else they will kill you and make her clean up your blood." Kelly pointed to Katrina. "Here." She tossed rags and a broom on the floor before finally leaving.

"It looks like she hates me. Is she that cold to everyone?" Alice grabbed the rags.

"Don't worry so much about her. We have a gift that we can use and no one can stop us." Katrina paused. She stared at the dirty floor beneath her feet. "Do you remember how we would clean our rooms after sleepovers?"

"I remember. It was fun, but your mother hated that we cheated." Alice laughed.

"Well this is almost like that!" Katrina stood on the bench and began to cast spell after spell. Soon there were cleaning supplies floating all over the room. Alice laughed at the silly rags dancing around the mirrors and the mops upside down on the ceiling, cleaning it completely. Soon, she got up and began to help with the process.

"I can see why you needed help," Alice teased. The girls held hands as the fingers on their other hands moved around and worked the cleaning supplies all over the bathroom. It didn't take them longer than twenty minutes to clean the gross bathroom and move onto the other seven in the camp. With each one their magic spells, they seemed to get stronger, along with their friendship.

Later that afternoon, Peter found Katrina in the laundry room. It was after she and Alice had finished their chores. They were helping other girls fold the clothing and prepare for the next group when they came. They were due in a couple of days. Alice was too busy too even notice him. She talked to another Jewish girl, who had arrived on the bus with her.

"I hate this place," Peter said.

"Why?" Katrina wrapped her fingers tightly into his.

"Because I can't enjoy you as much as I want to," Peter said. "If I could take you away from this hell and end the war, I would."

"That's a nice dream." Katrina gave a faint smile. They had the same wants, the same dreams. They were easy to grasp onto. Everyone there dreamed of something out of this place. But, it seemed nothing could free them.

Peter looked into Katrina's eyes. "I think I want to make you my wife." Before waiting for her to response, he placed his lips onto hers and took her breath away with the most love-filled kiss he could deliver. She flicked her tongue around the inside of his mouth. She thought of how they could be together and not fear death any longer. Then the reality hit her, she would always have fear. She wasn't mortal. She was a witch and witches were killed even more than Jews. And, they would continue to be killed. Would Peter love her, if he knew her darkest secret?

"I'll see you at dinner time." Peter walked away without another word. Katrina felt the linger of his lips on hers.

CHAPTER TWELVE

The sun was setting, that meant dinnertime in the mess hall. Without the evil Lion there, people were able to talk. There was even some light laughter at times. The fear of being called from the table and shot in the head for no reason was gone. The prisoners and guards were calm. And, with the Jews there now, there were more guards everywhere.

Peter stood by the chili pot making sure no one tried to take more than their allotted portion, or took too long getting food. Most of the new prisoners shook with fear. Peter gave them a calming smile. Many of them looked sick or close to death. Most likely, it was from fear. Everyone on the outside had heard of these camps and how Jewish people would be taken into special chambers to be killed or experimented on.

They feared that would be their fate. Peter wasn't an evil guard. He wanted to calm their fears as much as he could.

"At midnight. On the bench in the rear of the camp. Don't be late," Peter whispered as Katrina walked past him. Alice trailed behind her. He tilted his head slightly, trying hard not to draw too much attention to himself or Katrina.

"Who is he?" Alice whispered when they sat down next to Aunt Lisa. Alice had seen him earlier in the day, but didn't want to be nosy when it came to Katrina. Alice valued their friendship. Katrina was the one who stopped her death. The least she could do was mind her business.

"He's the one who protects her from the true hell of this place," said Aunt Lisa.

Katrina nodded. She sat down and they began to eat. Her aunt laughed when she saw Alice put the chili into her mouth then spit it out. "Oh, I need the spell for this food. Alice began humming lightly before dipping her spoon in the dish for another bite. Now, she could actually enjoy the dish she had no choice but to eat.

"You girls are done cleaning already?"

"No more left," Auntie," Katrina said. "With two of us the job is twice as fast, and dare we say, even twice as fun." She admired her aunt and loved her deeply. Even in this hellish place she still had the will to fake a smile. It was true, Aunt Lisa hated it there, but she covered her fears and feelings with a warm hug to any women who cried and a listening ear when anyone needed it.

The guards didn't bug Aunt Lisa. The guards didn't bug any of the quilters. As long as they were quiet, they'd be fine. All of them were older and didn't have much to say. They sat in their tent on simple, hard chairs and rocked their needles back and forth as they moved the fabric across their laps. There was a hum in the room as the women worked. Sometimes a guard would check in on them and maybe share a glass of water with them as well.

"I finished a quilt today. I've been feeling very tired lately. And my fingers have become numb from all the pokes," said Aunt Lisa. She showed the girls her sore fingers.

"Oh, no," said Katrina.

"The other quilters said to take a break for awhile since Lion wasn't here to beat me for it," said Aunt Lisa. The day was difficult. Aunt Lisa couldn't get the cries from her friends out of her mind. They had lost their children the day before because of Lion. And, the pain from her fingers began to dig deeper into her body. She was finding it difficult to stay positive, to want to live.

"Who's Lion?" Alice interrupted.

"The women who owns this place, we think. She killed twenty people for no reason the day before you came," Katrina said. "Including some a lot younger than us." Her voice shook, remembering. But, she worked hard to avoid making Alice cry. There was no time for tears right now when people cried every day in this place.

Alice gasped. "I hope you feel better Aunt Lisa." She placed her hand onto Aunt Lisa's hand and prayed for pain relief.

"I don't think magic will aid me on this issue," said Aunt Lisa. "But I admire your will and bravery to even try." Aunt Lisa went back to the sleeping tent, laid down and went to sleep.

The girls followed Aunt Lisa. "She's asleep, now what?" Alice said sitting on her cot.

"Let's talk for a while," said Katrina.

The girls talked and talked. The hours passed.

"Stay here. You'll be safe. Just be quiet. I have to meet Peter." Katrina smiled at her friend. She tried to push the wrinkles out of her dress. She wished she could have cleaned herself of the nasty smell of dirty bathrooms, but if she used magic, someone would notice she wasn't dirty or smelly.

"Does he know your secret?" Alice asked.

"No, and I'm nervous to tell him. You know how witches are treated these days." Katrina went to the doorway and looked toward the sky. The moon was full. She remembered her father saying that full moons make witches more powerful. It was all about the moon's glow and how it often matched the glow of a witch. She closed her eyes and remembered the time when he shared the story of how he admitted his gift to her mother.

"It was a dark night and the moon was so bright it could light a dark castle," he said. "I took her to a lake in the city. I even rented a boat so we could float into the middle and be in the moonlight. I wanted to show her something, so I asked if she'd close her eyes. I stood up and grabbed a tiny piece of a star from the sky. Only witches can do that, of course. I held it in my hand and told her to open her eyes. When she opened them, she screamed at the ball of fire in my hands. I told her not to worry. It was fine. Then I confessed my powers and the rest of the night she spent asking me questions. "

Katrina was so young and didn't understand it right then, but she did now. She wished she could do something as magical for Peter, but it wasn't something she could do in Camp Ravensbrook.

Alice came up behind Katrina. "Yeah, but witches aren't treated as bad as Jews are," Alice said. Her head hung low. She remembered the torture and the sights she had seen. Even other prisoners here hated her. She had even been pushed to the ground and kicked. If Katrina hadn't been there to stop them, she might have been dead. Alice was treated horribly. But, other Jews had it much worse at times.

"We can stop that, with magic," Katrina said.

"How can we without someone knowing we're witches?"

"By being selective and careful," Katrina said. She hugged her friend. "I'll do anything I can to save as many Jews and other prisoners from the pain of this Nazis camp. I won't stand for it. It's not right."

The other women became quiet. It was late and they were tired. Some of them eyed Alice as laid down to go to sleep. It was the perfect chance for Katrina to meet her promise.

"They will wake from their hatred. She is not evil. She is not bad. For this Jew is just like they. A trapped slave and nothing more. Be friendly. Be kind for she may bring thee the freedom thee desires." Katrina whispered her spell into the air. Alice hummed a sweet song to cover the words. All eyes were on them as a smoke of magic fell over the whole campsite and woke them from their hatred. Their evil faces turned to friendly faces.

"Thank you," Alice thought to Katrina.

"You're welcome," Katrina whispered. Then she walked out of the sleeping quarters. She waved a quick goodbye and drifted into the dark of night in hunt of Peter, trying not to be seen.

CHAPTER THIRTEEN

Katrina walked through the camp. Some of the guards stood half asleep, not really interested in their job. Some were alert and watched as she walked past, but did nothing about it.

It was because of Peter. He knew how to keep her safe. The guards knew Katrina was his and not to bother her.

"He's at the end of the camp," a guard said and pointed. There was a small tent in the corner at the farthest point in the camp. It was normally empty and used to hold supplies. Katrina walked slowly. As she got closer, she saw Peter laying on a bench outside the tent. The spot looked out onto the land outside the camp. The view was nice, but not far away were the bodies of those who were killed at the camp. The full moon removed a bit of the sadness Katrina felt.

"Hi," Katrina whispered. Peter smiled and got up. He motioned for her to sit next to him. They hadn't met there before and still felt shy and a bit awkward around each other. Katrina wasn't used to their relationship. Peter had to take things slowly to keep her calm.

"I brought you some sweet bread." He placed his hand into his side pocket then handed her a loaf of bread. He had been holding it for her since the morning. "I hope it's not stale."

Katrina smiled and kissed his check. "Thank you." She took a bite and although it was stale, it was delicious. She gobbled it up. It was the first food she'd eaten there that she didn't have to cast a spell over to enjoy. And, she got it from a man who she was falling in love with. The way he looked at her. The way he placed his hand into her hand, in the most tender way. He had love in his eyes, but he had yet to say the words to her.

"I saw you befriended one of the Jews," Peter said. Instantly Katrina prepared herself to defend her friend and run from him. "I'm glad you did," he finished saying.

A smile fell across her face. "You are?" She licked

her lips of the last few crumbs of the sweet bread. "But you're a Nazis."

"I am, but not by choice. I'm stuck here or I'd be killed as well." Peter lowered his eyes. "I'd rather be on the good side, but I don't have a choice."

"I knew her back home," Katrina said changing the subject. She was about to admit she was a witch, but stopped before she said anything. She didn't want to regret being honest just then. She didn't want to ruin the magic of the night they were sharing.

"I hate this place." Peter placed his arms around her.

Katrina wrapped her arms tightly around him. She barely felt the cold chill in the air because of Peter's strong arms holding her.

"I told you before, I can't enjoy you as much as I want to here," Peter said. "If I could take you away from this horror and end the war, I would. I want to make you my wife."

Katrina caressed him, thinking of how they could be together. Again, the fear entered her. It always came back. She wasn't mortal. She was a witch and witches were killed. "Your wife?" Katrina whispered.

"Yes. Would you marry a Nazis?" Peter smiled and leaned forward to kiss her lips once more.

"If that Nazis is you, I would. But you'd have to be an ex-Nazis by then," she teased. She pressed her body against his and kissed him with all the passion she had. The sweet bread had sent a charge in her body and made her want him. She had just been proposed to by the man she loved.

"You love me?" Peter looked into Katrina's eyes. The moon looked amazing behind her soft hair. Her eyes twinkled along with the warm smile on her face.

"I do." Katrina leaned forward to kiss him. Making love was new to them but it came naturally. They opened their souls to each other and welcomed their curiosity. Katrina moaned and hummed as their bodies combined and they enjoyed each other. "I love you," she whispered with every kiss he placed on her body. She savored the time they had alone and she savored him.

Then, reality set in. Katrina remembered she was a witch and he was a Nazis. The two of them were never supposed to be together. She was part of the Resistance. Yet, he didn't want to be in this hellish place either.

"Would you help me leave?" Katrina asked as they got dressed.

Peter looked at her. His eyes filled with fear. He didn't expect that. He wasn't prepared for a reply. "I don't know." He looked down. The smell from the dead bodies rose from the ground. He felt the urge to cry for their souls and for their families who lost them. "But, if given the chance, I'd help."

Katrina smiled and kissed him one last time before walking back to the sleeping quarters. The feeling of love filled her heart, but fear was in there with it. "I can make him more willing to help," she said to herself. "And, without magic." She promised herself she would.

Katrina laid in her bed next to Alice and remembered her mother's stories. There was a time when her mother would sing to her before she went to sleep. Other times her father would tell her sweet stories about young witches like herself. Katrina remembered one story in particular. It was about a young girl who was poor and wanted to use magic to solve all of her problems, so she did. With every wish she made, something good happened, but it didn't change her feelings, her outlook on life. Instead, she grew more and more needy. The problem was that with each wish, she became older. She became an old witch who was evil and lived in a dark home in the forest. And, it was all because of her greed and the act of using her magic to meet her greed.

"Katrina," her father would say at the end of the story. "While you have the gift of magic, you can't use it to solve all your problems. You are not God and cannot act like you are. Instead, you have to use your gift wisely. If you don't, you'll age quicker and become old, evil, and alone."

The words floated into Katrina's mind, as if her father was talking to her from the heavens. She didn't want to use magic to get out of the camp. She wanted to use her intelligence. She hoped someday she'd figure out just how to do it. But, right now, she would sleep and prepare herself for the next day of chores.

CHAPTER FOURTEEN

There were times in the morning when the sun rose just right and brought a smile to Katrina's face. Then she would look around and hear the cries of the women and children in pain. It turned her smile to tears. This was the place she had been forced to call home for the last three weeks.

Without Aunt Lisa, Alice, and Peter, Katrina didn't see herself lasting long. She didn't know how long she would be able to hold off from using all the magic in her soul to punish those who were punishing her and the other prisoners.

Every day, Jewish women and children were missing from the camp. This required Alice to stay close to Katrina at all times. If they weren't together, she too could be taken to the chambers that no one ever walked out of. Katrina knew what those chambers were: hell. They were the hell ruled by the Nazis party to rid the world of Jews. It was a horrific idea. The Resistance would stop it all. The Resistance would use the powers of all the witches in the world and save the Jews from this torture. Katrina knew it. She believed it. She had to, or else she would die from pure fear.

"Chores?" Alice said across from Katrina at the table. She looked into Katrina's eyes and could tell her friend was thinking deeply about something. "Or Peter?" she asked, wondering what held Katrina's attention.

"Actually, I was thinking about this hellish place and the insane plan the Nazis have," Katrina whispered in her mind. If she had spoken those words and a guard heard them, she'd be killed instantly. Katrina loved being able to talk to other witches without having to speak a word. It was amazing and gave her a sense of safety.

Alice shook her head. "I hope the Resistance stops this. It can't go on forever, that's for sure."

Katrina reached out and held Alice's hand. Tears made their way down Katrina's cheeks. The girls looked at each other. Even remembering their home was of no comfort.

A few tables away, a young Jewish boy and his mother sat. The boy was coughing and crying in his mother's arms. Like any good mother, she tried to console him, to make him feel better. Some of the older quilters were trying to help as well. But, when the boy began to throw up, it was apparent that he wasn't just sad or upset, he was extremely ill.

"Help! Help!" The mother cried out. A sick young Jew meant he couldn't work and that meant he couldn't be useful to the camp. That meant he would be killed. "I can't let him be sick!" the mother cried out. She looked sick also. Her whole body was covered in a rash, just like the child.

Alice looked up to Katrina and she smiled. "Should we?" she whispered into her friend's mind. They wanted to do something. They didn't want to simply say a pray that would allow him to die in peace. Instead, the girls wanted to heal him like their parents had taught them as little girls.

"I think we should at least try to help," Katrina said. She winked at Alice.

They found an empty bowl and went to the far corner of the lunchroom. "Soup. Bowl. Passion and love." The girls chanted together. "Liquid of red. Liquid of health. May thee be made whole." Inside the bowl, a red soup appeared unlike any other. It looked though like the gross chili they were given daily.

Katrina walked to the mother and whispered in her ear. "Do you believe in the Resistance?" she asked. The woman stopped crying and looked up. She saw Katrina. Alice came walking up behind Katrina with the bowl in her hands.

"I do," whispered the mother. "May the Resistance win."

"Then here." Alice handed her the bowl. "Let your son drink this. Then you drink it."

The mother gave the soup to her son. He drank a big portion. Then the mother drank the rest. The room fell quiet while the prisoners watched as the boy and his mother returned to health, right before their eyes.

"Believe in the Resistance." Alice whispered to the few women around them.

Katrina and Alice locked arms and walked slowly out of the hall. All eyes were on them. The prisoners knew better though, they quickly turned away. They knew if the guards noticed, Katrina and Alice would be killed.

"Did we just?" Alice screamed for joy once in the bathrooms where their magic cleaned. They had learned to speed up the process by holding hands and doing the same chant five or ten times instead of only three times.

"We did," Katrina said. "And it felt really great." She jumped up and twirled around the bathroom. "We could help everyone here and make this hell a little better place until the Resistance saves us all."

Alice laughed and danced around. "I agree. I hope you're right." Then she sat down on the bench in the middle of the bathroom.

"What's wrong?" Katrina said. "You've been sad most of the day. Even after we've just made that boy feel better."

"That's the thing. I'm a Jew," Alice said. "Last night I overheard some of the guards saying they hope to enjoy some Jews tomorrow night. I could be one of them."

"I won't let that happen." Katrina said. She made a fist and slammed it onto a stall door.

"You can't stop these jerks. And, neither can Peter. We're just slaves." Alice put her face into her hands and began to cry.

Katrina sat next to her friend and put her arms around her. "If the guards try to mess with you, I promise we'll use our powers to leave this place before it happens."

"You promise?" Alice said. "But what about Peter?"

"I don't need Peter. As much as I love him, I'm a witch of the Resistance and I must put that first." The words burned as they came out of Katrina's mouth. But, she meant every one of them. "We are strong. We will not let Camp Ravensbrook take our souls or our bodies."

"Could you also turn them into frogs if they try to rape me?" Alice asked. Her face was still wet with tears.

"If they try with you or me they won't know what hit them. And then if you'd like we can cook them in frog leg stew."

Alice laughed. "Lucky me. I love frog leg stew!"

CHAPTER FIFTEEN

The next morning women and children all over Camp Ravensbrook were sick.

Katrina did her chores with Alice. Neither said a word. She thought about her family and how much she missed her mother and father. She missed cleaning with them and she missed having silly fun in their backyard.

Tears pooled in her eyes as she waved her fingers around the large bathroom. She worked the brooms and mops while Alice cleaned the sinks and toilets. It was unusual for them not to talk and laugh. But, the weather was dreary and the illness all around them seemed to make the day depressing.

The girls finished their chores extra early, so went around the camp helping others with their chores. There were rumors going around about witches in the camp causing mischief. It made Katrina smile. Alice hung her head in fear of being discovered.

After helping others, Alice walked onto the mess hall line She smiled at the Jewish server behind the chili pot. "Hi," she whispered as she pushed her bowl forward and grabbed her serving of the nasty meal. She knew the moment she sat down she would turn it into tomato soup and cheese crackers.

Alice also missed her family. Her mother was an amazing and powerful Jewish woman. She was all heart and sweetness. She brought joy to even the saddest days and that joy was something Alice missed deeply. She wondered if her mother was laughing or singing in heaven while making lemon Jell-O in a large bowl.

Alice and Katrina sat to eat dinner next to Aunt Lisa. "I miss mine too." Katrina read Alice's mind.

"It's hard to be without them," Alice whispered.

"It is," said Aunt Lisa. She ate quickly and left, just as the guards were coming into the mess hall.

There were five or six guards and they laughed as they saw some of the women and children sick and unable to eat. Many couldn't lift their heads off the tables from all the work they had done during the day while being sick. Some were throwing up. When a young child threw up on a guard's shoe he kicked him. The child fell to the ground, helpless to do anything.

Katrina closed her eyes and used her strength to turn the bad into good. It was no use. There was too much bad for her to change it. She was just one witch and didn't have the power to change everything. She wanted to, but just then she couldn't.

She had to talk to Peter. She had to see if he was like these guards. Did he laugh at others who were sick?

Katrina got up. "I'll see you in the tent," she told Alice. She waved a quick bye and left. There, right outside the door, she saw the one thing she didn't want to see. Peter stood next to the guard tower laughing with another guard. They were laughing hard too.

What could be funny in this hell of a place? Death and the fear of a whip was all around. There was nothing funny about Camp Ravensbrook.

"Can I speak to you?" Katrina bowed when she approached him. A smile ran over his face. He spoke in German and told the other guard to leave them. She was his and only his. The guard looked over her dirty frail body, winked at Peter and walked away.

"I've missed you." Peter wrapped his arms around Katrina's slender waist. He pulled her into a soft gentle hug. If she hadn't been so mad at the time, she would have melted into his arms. He would have shielded her from the misery going on.

"How can you laugh in this place?" she nearly yelled the question. Katrina stopped herself before anyone could hear and come running to help Peter. He was a guard after all.

"What?" Peter said. "I was laughing at what?"

"I heard you laughing with the short guard. Laughing hard. Harder than the ones inside who care nothing about us."

"Why are you mad at me?" Peter pulled her close to him. "Talk to me."

"Because you aren't doing anything to stop this hell. You're just sitting back and letting them kill us all. Soon, I'll be one of them." She snatched her arm away from his.

"I'd never let that happen." His eyes burned with love for her. He would kill someone if he even considered touching Katrina. "I love you. Don't you understand that?"

"Fine! You love me. Who cares! I want freedom, not love!" Katrina's eyes blazed. "I want to love you, but not in a place where I have to worry that I'll be killed or someone I care about will be killed." Katrina wondered if this was a good time to tell him of her powers. She looked up into his eyes and saw the hurt growing in them. Instead of admitting her secret, she bit her lip and pushed her body into his.

"If you want freedom, I will do everything I can to give you that." He pressed his body against her and placed his finger on the bottom of her chin. He tilted her head up to his and pressed his lips onto hers. The energy of their love and passion surged between the two of them as they kissed.

They were too involved to care much about who was watching them. Instead, they just wanted to be with each other.

"I want to tell you," Peter said pulling his lips away from hers. "We were laughing about how I killed him at chess the other night and he didn't know why he lost so badly." He whispered in her ear, "I could never laugh about a place like this. But, with my job, I am forced to do what I must to fit in."

Katrina nodded and kissed Peter. Later that night, they met in a secret place that only they knew of. They made love and enjoyed each other's company. Talk of the future came up often, but Katrina changed the subject.

For some reason, she didn't see herself ever leaving Camp Ravensbrook. But, if she ever did, she knew she would make sure that Peter was by her side, holding her hand while they raced away.

CHAPTER SIXTEEN

Late night soon fell over the camp. It was a long day of chores and witnessing horrors. A quiet gossip hummed around the camp about what Katrina and Alice had done. The camp prisoners knew to keep it a secret for fear the guards might find out. The young Jewish boy was healthy and able to complete his chores. His mother was healthy and proud to believe in the Resistance for the first time since arriving there.

"You did that?" Aunt Lisa asked Katrina when she returned from her evening with Peter.

"Yes. Alice helped," she whispered.

Aunt Lisa smiled. "I'm glad to see that you are using your gifts to make the lives of those here better." She placed her hand on top of Katrina's "It's what makes us better witches."

Before Katrina could reply, her aunt closed her eyes and quickly fell asleep. Katrina's head slowly sunk into the hard pillow. It was just slightly less hard than the mattress below it. Comfort was not something Camp Ravensbrook cared to give its prisoners. It was nothing like the bed Katrina had when she was a child. Her bed, that the Nazis soldiers burned, was covered with soft pillows, dolls, and stuffed animals. And, it was outlined with hand-sewn lace from her grandmother. Tears fell from Katrina's eyes as she remembered. Her mother would play hide and seek in her room. She'd let Katrina win every time. Katrina would never have those days again. Instead, they'd be a distant memory.

Katrina hoped she would be able to sleep. After a long day of cleaning, the illness and gossip running through the camp, and the fact that she missed Peter, sleep didn't come. She wanted to sleep. No, she needed to sleep. She looked to her side. Her aunt slept, but not soundly. She grieved in her sleep to hide her sorrow during the day.

Katrina looked at Alice, who was almost rolled into a ball. Her head nearly touched her knees. She looked like a ball of hair. She too slept. She was blessed with the ability to fall asleep no matter how terrible the circumstances of her surroundings or circumstances. It was heartbreaking to look at her friend and know she was all alone. Katrina had her aunt at least. Alice had no one.

Fatigue settled into Katrina's body. She listened to the cries from nearby bunks. The itchiness from her clothes felt worse. She wished she could shower alone. She wished she could take a bath in a tub.

Katrina's hands trembled and her back screamed with every movement she made as she tried hard to get comfortable. Most of women and children in the tent were fast asleep. She was not yet one of them. She had to deal with it though. She had been at Camp Ravensbrook for over three weeks and hadn't been killed. This was an accomplishment. But, it felt as close to hell as anything could be. A fog slowly rolled into the tent and the dreams of freedom and escape rolled in with them. Some day, she and her aunt would leave this hell behind and the Resistance would win the war.

Just as Katrina eyes began to close with sleepiness, she heard yelling.

"Let them out!" a guard called from on top of one of the towers. Suddenly the sounds of barking could be heard.

"OH NO!" Katrina yelled. They had let the dogs loose.

Alice woke quickly. "This can't be for real." Many others in the tent woke up and began to cry from fear. Would the dogs come in there to chew on their bones?

"We can stop this," Katrina thought to Alice. Alice nodded. The two got up from their bed. They peered out of a small slit in the fabric and hoped the dogs couldn't smell their fear from a distance.

A pack of dogs, six or more, ran throughout the camp. On the towers, the guards watched and laughed. They wondered which young child would be dinner for the hungry monsters. Then the sound of a scream sounded over the barking as the dogs found their prey. They chased a young girl. She might have been only a couple of years younger than Alice. She could have been the age of the young girl who Lion killed days before. The girl ran and ran and ran, but not fast enough. The dogs were closing in.

The poor dogs were just hungry. A mixture of pit bulls and the scariest breeds ever created were included in the pack. They were thin from being starved. They were kept like that so they'd attack who or whatever they could find when let loose. This might have been their first chance of a meal in weeks. Their entire skeleton stuck out from their thinning fur. They had one focus and that was to eat.

The dogs drew closer and closer to the girl. The guards hung over the railing of the tower to see. They were still laughing. Their laughter only made Alice and Katrina madder. "What should we do?" Katrina whispered.

"Help her." Alice said.

"And them," Katrina said referring to the sick animals.

They watched as the girl's running began to slow and

the dogs were soon within perfect pouncing distance.

"Stop there now," Alice whispered into the moon. "Freedom. Passion. Stop. Breath. Fall." The young girl fell to the ground with a loud thump.

"Feed, but not on her. Full bellies. Thick fur. Now, be not mean. But lick, play and befriend," Katrina said. Instantly, the once ravenous dogs were full. They were no longer hungry. They barked at the girl, but instead of wanting to hurt her, they wanted to play. They began to lick her fingers and even her toes.

"Good job," Katrina said and placed her hand into Alice's. The two witches turned around and climbed back into the bed.

They heard the guards cursing. Other guards raced after the dogs to house them again. They cursed at the dogs and told the girl to get back to her tent. Their game of torture was over, with the help of two young witches. It was just the beginning, too.

CHAPTER SEVENTEEN

There were nights when things were simple and Peter would spend his time with Katrina. They talked and kissed in the light of the moon. But, this wasn't one of those nights. Peter's position had changed and many of the guards had gotten sick. It was very different than what he was used to.

Talk between guards caused a stir around the whole camp. It seemed that none of the evil punishments they had been using to torture the prisoners was working in the last month. It was driving the guards and those in charge crazy. They knew something was up, but couldn't figure out what.

"Those dogs are worthless. Stupid animals couldn't even kill the girl," said Captain Henry. "She got away with not a single bite on her." He sunk down into his chair and took off his hat, showcasing his thinning hair. He rubbed the top of his head and tried hard to laugh it off. "At least Lion wasn't here to see the stupidity of the whole thing."

"If she was here, the girl would have been shot instantly," said Gabriel, another guard.

"This bad luck keeps happening to us. Seems odd, doesn't it? Even the experiments didn't go well," the captain said.

"Maybe there are witches in the camp. Maybe they're using their powers to stop us," Gabriel said

Captain Henry nodded. "You might be right." Then the subject quickly changed to something else.

Peter sat in the corner of the guard's quarters,

drinking a bottle of beer and trying hard to get Katrina out of his mind. He was in love with her and not seeing her daily was starting to take a toll on him. He wanted to see her. He wanted to kiss her. He wanted her. Sadly, his new position took all his time. Fun was out of the question.

Peter's new position was to watch the male Jewish prisoners on the other side of the town, in a different camp. He was forced to watch as the men did backbreaking chores, like breaking rocks or digging graves for the many dead bodies that rested between the two camps. It was another form of hell. The men didn't cry like the women, but they did show their pain and hatred for it all. Peter held onto a whip daily, but never used it. Their chore was punishment enough. At least he thought so.

In the guard's quarters, he began to wonder what the other guards were talking about. From the sounds of it, there really might be a witch in the camp causing trouble. Things that should work smoothly seemed to be going awry. From the sick guards, to the dogs not attacking, and then the experiments going wrong. Something was off. Something just wasn't right.

His mind drifted back to Katrina. She was his heart suddenly. It seemed like he had purpose in this camp when she was around.

"There is something wrong out there. Come help me Peter," Tim, another guard said as he raced into the quarters and then raced back out. Peter rushed to catch up with him. "It seems there's a fight among some of the girls in a tent," said Tim.

Alice heard the fight, but didn't want to wake Katrina. She knew Katrina hadn't been sleeping well. Instead, she got up and went on the hunt for the source of the crying and yelling. It didn't sound like someone was being hurt, it sounded more like two women fighting.

Alice came close to the tent and peaked in a hole. She saw Peter and another guard inside the tent trying to get the two young women apart.

"What's this fight about!?" Tim yelled.

Many of the other girls in the tent tried to sleep through the ruckus, but it was impossible. Instead, they angled their heads to the side and listened with closed eyes.

"She put a star of David on the bottom of her pillow!" the taller women said.

Alice gasped at the idea. She wished she had been brave enough to do something like that, but she wasn't. Alice admired the shorter women who stood across from the taller older one. She was brave. She wasn't afraid of being punished because of her faith.

"I don't want this Jew in my tent any longer!" the taller women yelled.

Peter stood between them to keep them from touching each other. "It's not that simple. We could easily take you both to the chamber and you won't have to worry about such things." He said the words, but there was no feeling in them. He didn't even remove his whip from the back of his belt.

"Or, we can just whip them until they're too sore to do anything," Tim said. Then he laughed. "I haven't used my whip all day. Maybe I should use it all night on you two for ruining our peace and quiet."

Peter tensed his body. He tried to think of something to say to keep Tim from whipping the shorter women. "We don't need to go that far. Listen to me."

"I can't promise I will listen to the crap you say," Tim said.

Alice watched as the Jewish young woman stood very still and quiet. She didn't talked at all since the guards came into the tent. And, for good reason too,

Tim was very much against the Jews and might have killed her simply because of the sound of her voice. Peter would have tried to defend her, but he wasn't as ruthless as Tim. And, he couldn't obviously try to defend an Jew.

Alice had to think quickly. She couldn't let them punish either woman. And, she especially didn't want the Jewish girl to be punished just for being Jewish. "She shall speak and they will listen," Alice whispered.

Tim opened his mouth to speak, but stopped. He pulled his whip from his back, but didn't strike either girl. Instead, he just held it. "I'll take your pillow, he said to the Jewish girl. You can sleep without one." He bent down and grabbed the pillow. As he walked out of the tent he scratched his head. He wasn't sure why he didn't whip the girl, like he wanted to. He shrugged it off though.

The Jewish woman lowered her head. "Am I going to be in trouble, sir?"

"No," Peter said. "But I think you may want to find someone on the other end of the tent to trade beds with tomorrow to avoid this from happening again."

"Good, I can't wait to get rid of her!" the taller women said.

Peter looked at the taller woman. "You should be careful too. You all could be dead tomorrow no matter what race you are. We are under the control of Hitler and whatever he says goes. If he decided to kill large young women with blond hair and brown eyes, you'll be the first to go." Peter walked out. He didn't notice Alice standing on the side of the tent. He walked right past her.

Alice's mouth hung open. She had never heard him speak like that before. He wasn't mean. He just warned them to behave. And, it was a truthful warning.

Alice raced back to her own tent. Peter went back to the guards' quarters and Tim went back on patrol.

"Where did you go?" Katrina said when Alice got back. "Are you okay? Was it another guard...?" Katrina instantly assumed it was an evil man trying to take advantage of her best friend.

"No. No. Nothing like that," Alice said quickly. She smiled and got into bed. "I heard a fight and went to investigate. It was between two young women."

"Oh, did the guards catch you?" said Katrina.

"Almost. Peter was there and another guard named Tim."

"Oh. Tim. He's the cold, mean one," Katrina said putting her nose up into the air. "I can't stand him."

"Nobody can." Alice said. Then she leaned closer to Katrina. "I used my magic to make it better for all of them," she whispered. Then she told Katrina everything that went on. She spoke in thoughts though, to avoid anyone hearing them talk about magic and their gift to help people.

"Thank goodness. The Jew might have been killed had you not stepped in. If not killed, she could have been whipped or beaten," Katrina said. "I'm glad you helped them." The two girls hugged before they fell asleep.

CHAPTER EIGHTEEN

The sun slowly rose and the fresh air from the surrounding forest seeped into the tent. But, the sunlight and fresh air quickly turned to horror. Everyone was awaken in the worst possible way.

Three mean guards walked into every tent and began to bang and stomp on everything they could. They even flipped over some mattresses.

"Get up you stupid losers!" a balding guard with a fat stomach yelled at the top of his lungs. Another guard began to push and pull the women out of the tent.

"We have a show for you," said a young guard. His eyes locked onto Alice's for a moment. He smiled at her. Then he saw the "J" written on her shirt to note that she was a Jew. His smile turned evil and he began to push her.

He might have pushed her to the ground if Katrina hadn't been there to hold onto her hands and pull her out of the room quicker.

"Thank you, Katrina," Alice whispered to her best friend. "I wonder what's going on."

"Knowing these jerks, they aren't going to take us to a nice show and give us freshly made popcorn while we drink lemonade," Katrina said. Popcorn and lemonade. She daydreamed about it often. There was something about the salty buttery treat that crunched in her mouth. And, the sweet and sour taste of chilled freshly made lemonade caused her to smile. Even when she was crying inside for the freedom she craved, the thought of lemonade and popcorn made her smile.

Katrina shook her head and the thoughts of her favorite treat disappeared. She and the others stood and waited for the next orders the guard would give. "Look," she whispered to Alice. In the spot where busses dropped off prisoners, a tall, heavy guard with platinum hair stood with a whip in his hand. Next to him was a young female prisoner.

The whip was bigger than any other whip they had seen before. It was thick and could cause serious harm to anyone who was in its way. Katrina shivered at the idea of the woman being hit with it. Katrina looked at the woman. She looked as if she was drop dead gorgeous before the war. The young woman had golden hair and beautiful face. She wasn't a new prisoner though. Her clothing and body were dirty. Then Katrina looked down. She gasped to herself when she saw the baby bump. This new prisoner had to be close to six months pregnant. Katrina wondered if a guard was the father or if she was pregnant on arrival.

"She's pregnant," Katrina thought to Alice.

Alice's eyes opened wide. "Oh, no."

The girl's head hung so low it touched her chest. Her body and legs were tied to a large steel pole that the guards must have just placed there. Her arms were tied above her head. It looked like the most uncomfortable position possible.

"Attention!" the platinum haired guard said. His voice carried all over the courtyard. Everyone stopped talking and listened. He cleared his throat. He held his whip slightly behind his back, ready to strike her.

"This women is an example of what you should never be! Unless, you want the same fate as her. She slept with a guard and was caught stealing from our pantry. This snake actually made off with a dozen carrots and tried to smuggle them to the other prisoners. We're not stupid! We're guards and we punish those who need it! This morning, you will all learn what happens when you steal from us. Let this be the worst type of reminder to any Jew or other prisoner of what not to do." There was a smile on his face as he whipped the air to show just how powerful the weapon in his hand was. The crack sounded like a cannonball. It could kill the poor girl. Alice tensed up and tried to hold back her tears.

"Do you think we can help stop this?" Alice thought to Katrina.

"We can at least try. Maybe lessen her pain, or stop it completely," Katrina thought back.

They locked hands, intertwining their fingers as they focused their powers onto the guard. The guard raised his whip. He had a wide smile on his face. Katrina and Alice's eyes grew wider as they worked their magic to bring him the same fate Katrina had done to the men raping the girls a couple of weeks earlier.

Suddenly, the guard grabbed his stomach and his ass, dropping the whip to the ground. He raced away in hopes of finding a bathroom before it was too late. Unfortunately for him, it was too late. There was a dark brown stain all over his pants and it got worse as he ran.

"He won't be back for awhile," Katrina thought to Alice. She was right.

Most of the guards walked away after an hour of waiting for the guard to return. A couple of the other guards took the girl off the beam. Word was they took her back to her camp and she was made to break bricks throughout the night as punishment.

The next day, rumors ran around that camp that the girl was shipped off to a camp that housed pregnant girls. They didn't know what would happen to her. Alice assumed it'd be okay, since she wasn't a Jew. Katrina didn't have the same outlook, but did hope for the best.

CHAPTER NINETEEN

Even with the harsh conditions in Camp Ravensbrook, there was one little Jewish boy who was a shining beacon for all the prisoners. His name was Joel. He was close to seven years old, but the size of a tall toddler, simply because he was unfed and overworked like the rest of the prisoners. Joel would frolic around the courtyard, waving his arms. He had a free-spirited nature. He'd smile and sing Jewish songs he sang during the holidays. He'd even tell jokes. Even in their dimmest days, when it seemed like the guards were just trying to make hell worse, Katrina and Alice would crack a small grin whenever they saw him. For someone who was rail-thin, he could run nonstop, and even the strongest guards stumbled to catch him.

"It seems pretty quiet right now," Alice said as they looked around the mess hall, enjoying the meals they witched-up. Alice dipped her spoon into the large bowl of gross warm chili, but in her mouth it was warm cream of broccoli soup, and the best she had ever had.

"It seems like a few people are missing from the hall," Katrina said. She gestured to the nearby tables and noted that it seemed each table was missing three or four people. There were mothers who didn't have their children nearby and vice versa.

I hope it's not Lion doing her thing," Alice said. "I could be next if so."

Katrina placed her hand onto Alice's. Fear had been building in their bodies. They knew something would happen soon. No matter what anyone thought, something bad would happen to the Jews in this camp. They just had to avoid it the best they could.

After lunch, Katrina and Alice walked from the mess hall. They finished their chores and planned on going to the quilters' tent to see if there was anything they could do. It was truly the only safe place in the whole camp. Many prisoners went there just for peace and quiet and, most importantly, safety.

Across from the quilters' tent stood a large brick building. It was tall and didn't seem to fit into the camp. All the other buildings were tents or smaller wooden buildings. The girls never saw anyone go into it. It was just there. As the girls were about to enter the quilter's tent, the door of that building flew open. Joel walked out. Katrina smiled as she expected him to race towards them and begin to play a game of hide and seek under the quilts the ladies were working on. Instead, he stumbled out.

His fingers were cracked and stuck in odd positions. His head tilted to the side. He dragged his leg behind him. It didn't seem to move on its own. He looked as if he was drugged or a zombie.

When Joel reached the girls, he glanced at them with glazed eyes that didn't seem to blink. His skin was a bright red and covered with a scaly rash. Drool seeped from his mouth. He tried to say something, but his words were mumbled.

"What's wrong with our little light?" Alice asked. She often called him that.

Katrina didn't bother replying. Instead, she grabbed Alice's hand and headed toward the large building Joel just came out of. Thankfully, no guards were around. None were needed there. No one in his right mind would venture in. Katrina looked around. She slowly grabbed the door. "Come on," she told Alice.

Alice looked behind her, making sure no one saw them entering the building. Katrina held onto Alice's hand. Slowly, cautiously, then went in.

It was nothing like they thought it would be. There were large fluorescent lights that dangled from the ceiling. And, there were closed doors all along the dark dingy corridor. At the other end of the building, the girls could see an open door. They heard screams. There was broken glass all over the hallway and there was a thick black disgusting liquid on the floor.

Katrina and Alice had to be very careful of each of their steps, so not to get cut by the glass. But, as careful as they were, there were too many pieces to avoid. They ignored the pain and continued on, until they were in front of the open door. They hugged the wall, hoping not to be seen.

"Stay down stupid!" someone ordered. "Grab her and keep her down," he yelled at the guards. Katrina's eyes widened as they peered around the edge of the doorway.

Three guards strapped a young women to a dilapidated chair. A man with a black hat, large beard, and wearing a lab coat paced the room. He carried a syringe filled with a bright red liquid. The needle looked rusted and ready to break apart. It wasn't something a doctor would use. It wasn't something that would be used on an animal. It wasn't a needle that should be put into a person.

Alice covered her mouth and gasped. She saw the "J" written on the very top of the prisoner's shirt. The young woman in the chair was Jewish. Alice trembled as she thought about her own body in that chair. Could she be the next to be strapped down?

"Hold still!" the doctor demanded as he went to the woman. Even with the guards pinning her down, she still convulsed and dodged his attempts to inject her.

She was a smart young woman and didn't want to be a test subject for these jerks. She was doing everything she could to avoid that needle.

Katrina recalled the conversation she had overheard others talking about in the tent one evening.

"I heard they're testing out a drug this week," a young boy said to another.

"Yeah, but only on the Jews," a girl replied.

"Then we don't have to worry," the boy said.

The thought of them testing something on Jews made Katrina's blood boil. She looked behind her and saw Alice down on the floor in tears.

Alice firmly believed she'd be next. She knew they would do whatever they could to rid the world of Jewish people. This was just their first step.

Rumor had it that Dr. Wilt was testing a drug on Jews in the hopes of catching witches in the process. With all the magic happening around the camp, something had to be done to rid the camp of magic. The guards assumed that any witches at the camp were Jewish. If they used their drug on the Jews, the magic would stop too.

Katrina shuddered and began to cry. This was her fault. She was to blame for the use of the drug. She and Alice had been working their magic to better the camp. Instead of making it better, they were causing hell to happen a hundred times worse. The guards were on alert and so was Lion. This was horrible.

Katrina knelled next to Alice and hugged her tight. "I'm sorry," she whispered into Alice's ear. "It's my fault."

Alice began to cry quietly into Katrina's shoulder. The sounds of the screaming girl hid their cries of sorrow. "We have to stop them," Alice declared. "I've been practicing my magic and I'm much better at it now. Let me try."

Katrina backed away as Alice peered into the room. The guards had finally strapped the young women down. The man, most likely Dr. Wilt, held the syringe, ready to inject it. He smiled.

Alice glanced around. She saw a shelf filled with vials containing liquid that looked similar to what was in the syringe. With her right eye, she concentrated on the shelf. With her other eye, she fixated on the syringe. Witches could move their eyes independently. Her eyes widened. In a flash, the syringe and all the vials on the shelf exploded. Glass flew everywhere, and the liquid seeped from the shelves.

The suddenness of what happened caused the guards to let go of the girl. The doctor stood there with his jaw unhinged. Katrina and Alice sprinted across the corridor, out the door, and sped to one of the bathrooms. Thankfully, there were no guards around.

"That was a close one," Katrina panted as they finally began to relax.

"At least we stopped them," Alice said. She paused and looked down. "For now at least."

"Yeah, but what if the doctor and guards think the girl about to be injected did it? said Katrina. "Who knows what they'll do? And, we're just delaying the inevitable. They'll get more drugs."

"Then we'll destroy those as well," Alice replied.

Katrina sighed. "We have to destroy this whole place. Not just by doing small things. The Resistance has to beat these jerks now, not later."

"I'm ready when you are." Alice narrowed her eyes. "Now all we need is a plan."

CHAPTER TWENTY

The girls went back to their tent. Katrina sat on the edge of the small cot; her heart was heavy. Next to her lay Aunt Lisa. She was pale and didn't look well. She was unable to move or get up. It seemed like she was near death.

There had been sick people all over the camp. Women were dying daily. But, Katrina never thought Aunt Lisa would be one of those to get sick and die in this place. She didn't see this happening. They were supposed to leave together, locked in arms. They were to be together forever.

"We have to get medicine," Alice said to the other girls in the tent. They all gathered around Aunt Lisa. While it would just be another death, each and every one tore at their hearts. They hoped that some kind of prayer or even witchcraft would help, but it seemed even the strongest of witches couldn't stop this death.

There were rumors around the camp that medicines were available for the sick in other camps. It was even in Camp Ravensbrook, but only for those in charge and the guards. Katrina would ask Peter often why the camp had no medicine for the prisoners. He had no answer. He was after all, just a guard.

It killed Katrina that she couldn't do something. She wanted desperately to have medicine for Aunt Lisa. The guards didn't care if people died from being sick or from being tortured. They would just take their bodies and throw them away like trash.

"They're coming to pick people," a young girl said.

"Lie down and pretend to be asleep." She hopped in her bed.

Katrina moved quickly and so did Alice. They didn't bother asking questions. It was pointless to think a young girl would lie when life was in the hands of these ruthless people. A guard entered the room. He shined his large flashlight all over the beds. He saw two older girls in the corner with their eyes half open and picked them up by their hair. He then dragged them out of the tent. The girls struggled and cried, but no one could help them.

"Should we?" Katrina thought to Alice.

"I don't want us to get caught. We could get into serious trouble," Alice replied.

When the guard finally left, they sat up. Katrina went back to her aunt. She held her hand while Alice walked over to the young girl to ask what was going on.

"Have you heard the bombs?" the girl said.

Katrina and Alice nodded. Everyone in the camp heard them nightly. Sometimes as many as six bombs in a single night.

"What about them?" Alice asked. She swallowed hard as she prepared to hear the truth. She didn't want to hear it, but her curiosity made it hard to avoid.

"They use women and children to detonate bombs. It's a way to kill more of us and stop the Resistance's advances." The girl looked down.

"I can't believe it," Katrina said, holding her aunt's hand as she dozed off to sleep.

"I know. It's depressing," the girl said. "They take them, give them vests fitted with bombs all over, and then tell them they're free. When the guard tracking them radios back that they're close to the enemy, the bombs are set off. It kills the women and children and the intended target."

Alice shock her head. A chill ran through her body. "That's just horrible."

"Nothing about this place is right," Katrina said. "And there is nothing we can do to stop it."

The young girl laid down in her bed. "At least for tonight we hold onto our own lives. Tomorrow is another day of chance." She soon fell asleep.

"Could we do magic to stop that?" Alice said

"We aren't strong enough. We couldn't make it stop from this distance. And, we can't stop the bombs without seeing them."

"Then it's hopeless." Alice began to weep. "Your aunt is dying because of this place and even with all the good we've done, it's not enough."

Katrina hung her head. "We've done what we can do. It's not like we have to stop. We just can't do it all."

"We have to think bigger. We have to leave this place," Alice said. "Maybe if we get your aunt out of here she'll live."

"Maybe," whispered Katrina. But, her face had worry all over it. She feared there wasn't hope for her aunt. She feared Aunt Lisa would die soon. "The only way she might live is if we could get her to the Resistance. They could help."

Alice got into bed. "She can still move a little. We can take her. I promise. We'll try to do everything we can to take her away from this place."

"I hope you're right," said Katrina. She was at a lost for any other words. She wasn't sure what she could do. She got up from the bed just as Alice began to sleep. She walked around the camp, hunting for Peter. She knew he would lift her spirits. All she had to do was see him. As she walked, she sang soft songs of magic that made tiny stars fly between her fingers. She remembered when her father would make the stars fly at night after a bad day. The sight always made her smile.

Suddenly, the sound of a breaking twig startled her.

"What are you doing?" Peter said from behind her. "Was that magic?" He looked so mad. He looked evil. He looked like the other guards.

"I'm a witch. I'm part of the Resistance." Katrina tried to hold her body strong. She didn't want to cry. She wanted to hug him. She wanted to kiss him. But, she knew right then he would only push her to the ground and maybe even spit on her for lying to him all this time.

"I can't believe you never told me!" he yelled. His voice brought the women in the tents nearby to their doorways to listen. He pulled her from there, but not in the gentle way he usually did. Instead, he grabbed her arm like she was an animal and carried her to the darkest part of the camp, far past the testing building. "Explain," he ordered.

"How could I tell you? Would you have listened, or would you have had me killed like the others?" Katrina said. "It doesn't change anything between us."

"Don't you think better of me? I would never have you killed. But, lying to me isn't helpful." Peter said as he paced.

"I only lied to protect my family." Katrina tried to touch him. She wanted to remind him of the way they melted into each other.

"No, you lied to keep me from having you turned in and killed. You're part of the Resistance. You're the reason there is a war," he said

"I am part of the Resistance, but this war is because of Hitler and the Nazis army. It's not because of me! Don't blame me for the death they've caused that could have been avoided."

"You may be right about that one. But, this isn't the

type of love I want. It's not an honest love." Peter turned his back to Katrina.

"This is because you don't trust a witch. It's not like I could have told you in between our kissing or times alone. Peter, I've fallen in love with you and I don't want to lose you because of something I can't control. I'm not some evil witch. I've worked to help and protect the prisoners here."

Peter turned back to face Katrina. "This can't work. This won't work. We can't do this. You're a witch. And that's just not going to work." Peter's face was red. He wasn't able to think straight. He looked into her eyes and wondered what had happened. "Did you use your evil powers to make me love you? You did! You must have!" Peter stormed off, shaking his head. Tears fell from his eyes. He had to walk away. He never wanted to return to this woman. If he did return to Katrina, would he still feel love for her or pure hated for the lying witch blood within her body?

"I'm a witch, but I'm still the same Katrina who you stopped from being whipped," she called after him. "I never did that to you. I never used my gift on you."

"No, you are not the same Katrina I fell in love with. You're the one stopping the guards from doing their jobs to make yourself feel better." Peter was almost gone from Katrina's sight.

"I'm not!" Katrina called to him. "I didn't do that. I love you Peter!" She fell to her knees and began to sob.

He was her last hope and now he was gone. She lost her mother and her father. And, soon her aunt would be gone. All within a month. Now, the only person who gave her faith that this war would end was also gone. Her body trembled as the reality set in. She felt lost and alone and wondered if she would be killed for being a witch.

CHAPTER TWENTY-ONE

The next morning Katrina's aunt's health worsened. There was nothing she could do but beg for the medicine. She couldn't even think about the fight she had with Peter the night before. It was pointless to think about it when he was furious with her.

Lion was in the camp. She arrived that morning. Peter's uncle had told her that some of quilters were dying. She came to see for herself. She walked into the camp wearing all white. She wore bright teal blue shoes and a blue ribbon around her red hair to match. She held a whip in her hand and hit the air when anyone stepped in her way while on the way to the quilters' room.

"Can you help my aunt, Ma'am?" Katrina bowed low to show respect for this evil woman. She would have kissed the bottom of Lion's feet if it meant her only relative would live. Katrina's effort did nothing to soften Lion. Instead, she smiled in the evilest way and touched Katrina's arms to lift her from the ground.

"If a quilter dies, she must die." Lion's bright red lipstick made it easy to want to punch her in the face. "There is nothing we can do."

"But, we have the medicine to make her live," Katrina said.

"Please let us help her," Alice begged.

"Silence or I will kill both of you with a shot to the heart." Lion pointed down to the gun on her side. Katrina remembered the day before Alice arrived and the sadness that filled the camp when this evil woman caused harm.

The girls looked down at the floor and locked hands instead of looking into the eyes of hell.

"I thought you'd changed your mind," said Lion. I'll allow you to bury her away from the other dead bodies because she was a good quilter after all." Lion walked away with a cackle of laughter behind her. All the quilters in the tent came to Aunt Lisa's bed. They all put their hands onto her sick body. Praying for her.

"Hold tight," they moaned. They wished the pain away, wanting her to have a pain free passing.

Katrina cried. She couldn't hold back her tears. She could not hold back her hatred of the hell she was in either. She cried and prayed. She cried and held on to her aunt.

Soon, Aunt Lisa's eyes opened wide and she took her final breath. "I love you, Katrina. Be good my dear child" she whispered. Then she was gone.

Katrina fell to the ground. Alice wrapped her arms tightly around Katrina and held her as she wept. Alice tried hard to hold herself together. Katrina had now lost everyone in her family.

"Why? Why? Why?" Katrina screamed out. She cried harder than she ever had before. She felt lost. She felt alone.

"We have to get out of this hell," Alice thought to Katrina.

"I know," said. Katrina. "And we have to do it before the month ends or they will kill us too. I feel it."

The others weep softly. They helped Katrina carry Aunt Lisa away from the other bodies. The bodies that were thrown away like trash. Aunt Lisa wasn't trash or dirt, neither were the others. But, Katrina had the okay for Aunt Lisa to be placed in a proper grave, at least something like a proper grave for Camp Ravensbrook.

Katrina went through the motions, but couldn't feel anything. They walked past the other bodies. She noticed the faces of the dead women and children who were killed by the Nazis guards. Katrina stopped walking. "I can't. I don't want to say goodbye."

"Then say 'see you in heaven,'" one of the quilter's said, as they placed Aunt Lisa onto the ground and piled fresh daisies on her chest and crossed her palms over them.

Katrina nodded. She bent down onto the ground and kissed the forehead of her aunt. "I will see you in heaven, Aunt Lisa," she whispered. "And I'll make sure the Resistance wins." Illness didn't matter. Death didn't matter. Chores had to be done. And, Katrina and Alice had to work on their plan to escape.

"We have to get out of this place," Alice said while the brooms worked to clean the bathroom and the sponges danced in circles all around the room.

Katrina had been quiet for hours. They buried her aunt in a shallow grave. They placed lots of flowers on top and even the quilting square she had been working on before her death. Katrina was heartbroken.

"Yes, we do," said Katrina. But, there is no way we can do it alone." She sighed deeply and sat on the bench. Her loss felt overwhelming. "I have to tell Peter everything and hope he forgives me," she said.

"I can take care of that. I know Peter loves you." Alice tried to laugh for Katrina's sake. "The whole camp knows he loves you. It's not a deep dark secret. He can't stop loving you just because you can make brooms dance and people feel better."

Katrina sighed and looked up at her best friend. Alice was trying so hard to make her feel better and it was slowly working. If not for Alice, Katrina might have been completely hopeless without her Aunt. But, her best friend stood beside her, held her hands, and was a shoulder for her to cry on when the pain of death came her way. She was truly a gift and a gift she cherished more than anything right now. "I hope you're right, Alice."

"I'm always right!" Alice said and she made the sponges dance in a small circle above their heads. They danced in a pattern almost like swimmers in the ocean. It was the first time in hours that Katrina was able to muster up a tiny smile.

"I miss my aunt. I miss my mother. I miss my father," Katrina said. "But you know, I'm really glad we are together." She hugged her best friend tightly.

CHAPTER TWENTY-TWO

That night, Katrina couldn't sleep. She sat on her cot looking up at the very top of the tent. There were bugs all over the tent and dozens of cobwebs covering the corners. But, it was all she had. Her eyes were tired. Her body was tired. Her small thin pillow under her face was soaked from her tears. As exhausted as she was, she couldn't sleep.

When she closed her eyes she'd see her aunt staring back at her, holding the hand of her father. Then she would blink and see Peter storming away, like he did the day before her aunt died. Katrina felt she had nothing. Her heart ached. Her soul ached. She had no family and the man she fell in love with inside the hellish camp, had discovered her secret. And, now, he didn't want anything to do with her.

Katrina moaned. She tossed and turned in the small bed. She wept and wept and wept. Still, sleep wouldn't come. She needed to walk. She needed a break from the sadness of the empty bunk next to her. Katrina got up from the bed and tiptoed out of the tent. Alice was snoring deeply, like she always did.

There were a few guards out and most of them knew who she was. They knew that she was Peter's and often ignored her when she walked around the camp in search of him. They might not have known about the recent break up. That was okay with her for now. With luck, she might even see him and get a chance to explain herself.

Katrina walked and walked. But, she had no idea where she was headed. Then she saw a tent with a light on inside. She heard Lion. She moved closer and closer to the tent, almost as if she was being guided there. Maybe, her father sent a gift to motivate her to spy on them. Her sleepiness faded. She had to find out what was going on.

Katrina placed her ear to the rough fabric and listened. There was a lot of mumbling at first, but after a quick spell, she was able to hear the words clearly and see through the material.

"I think we should kill everyone in the camp." Lion crossed her legs as she sat in the captain's chair. The captain kneeled before her. He wasn't worthy enough to sit beside her. The camp was falling apart because there were witches in it.

"But, ma'am," he said. His body was tense. His voice sounded as if he were scared. Maybe Lion had used her whip on him.

"Silence," said Lion." It seems that with every task I give you, a witch gets in the way."

"We tried to stop them with the chemical you gave us," Captain Henry pleaded.

Lion laughed. She actually laughed like a hyena. It was evil sounding. "And, that didn't work at all! Have you seen what happened to those things? You let that stupid witch ruin all the chemicals we had." She paused for a moment to light a cigarette.

"We can't just kill them all," said Captain Henry. "It'd take too long. There are plenty of chores for them to do that will kill them slowly." He was trying to save his job, not the women and children at the camp.

"We don't have time to kill them slowly," Lion said. She paused to take a smoke from the cigarette in her long fingers. The captain coughed as Lion blew the disgusting smoke directly into his face. "Can't you tell by now that I don't like waiting?"

Captain Henry stood on his feet. "Yes, ma'am. Then what would you like us to do?"

"Take them in groups of fifty into the gas chamber tomorrow. I want this whole camp killed by the end of the week." Lion laughed. "Do you understand?"

"Including the ones that aren't Jewish?" asked the captain.

"No one should be alive after Friday." Lion got up and pulled him to her face. "Do I make myself clear?"

Captain Henry swallowed hard then nodded. "Yes, ma'am.

Lion got up and left.

Lucky for Katrina, Lion didn't see her standing beside

the tent, listening to everything they said.

"They're going to kill all of us starting tomorrow," Katrina whispered to herself, not really believing it for a moment. She wasn't so much worried as she was furious. She wasn't going to let that horrid woman kill her. She didn't want to let her win that right to take her soul and claim it as her own.

Katrina began to walk back to her tent. She avoided going on the same path she had taken there. The path she took was a dark one and one she didn't remember being on before. There were tents on either side and it seemed inside of them people were coughing nonstop.

"What the hell are you doing out of your tent?" A guard pulled on her from behind. "A little girl like you should be sleeping, not walking around this late at night."

"I just got up to get some water. I can't find my way back to my tent. I'm sorry, sir." Katrina whispered the words and tried to tremble as if she were sick.

The guard could sense she wasn't sick. "I can give you some water." An evil grin creep onto his face. "You aren't one of those sick ones are you?"

Katrina began to fake a cough. "I am…"

The guard grabbed her arm and dragged her away from the tents.

"I doubt that. You seem too pretty to be sick." He placed his hands on top of her head and rubbed them into her dirty hair. Then he placed his nose on her head and smelled her. "And if you are, I really don't care." He dragged her into a small empty tent. "Get on your knees," he ordered.

"I just want some water," Katrina said.

"You can have water afterwards." He laughed as he began to undo his pants.

Katrina wasn't stupid, nor was she the type of woman to let this guy take advantage of her. "I think you should let me go," she insisted. She didn't cry like most girls did. Instead, she just stared at him.

"Oh, and what's going to happen if I don't?" he asked.

"I'll turn you into a frog and step on you." She looked into his eyes.

"You can't do that. You're just some Jew with no soul," he said.

"I'm not Jewish. But I am a witch," Katrina said. She closed her eyes and her energy pushed him down to the floor. He let out a German curse word the moment he fell. Katrina got up and floated into the air. She was so mad her anger ignited her power and gave her the energy of all her family members. She pointed at him with her finger. That's all she did. She didn't speak.

She pointed and a magical light came from her finger.

"Don't!" he started to say, but it was too late. The next sound that came from his mouth was the sound a frog made.

She floated back down to the ground and walked slowly over to the frog sitting on the floor. "I warned you," she said. She picked him up and held him in her hands. "You can't try to rape a witch. We turn foul people into frogs. Understand?"

The frog tried to nod, but instead its tongue flew into the air as a fly went pass them.

Katrina placed the frog into her pocket and walked back to the tent. She hoped no one would notice the missing guard until the morning. But, at this point, she really didn't care. They were planning to kill everyone in the camp, starting tomorrow. This meant Katrina had to do something tonight. She had to wake up Alice and tell her everything.

Katrina snuck back into her tent. She shook Alice. "Wake up."

"It can't be morning yet," Alice said as she turned over.

"It's not." Katrina pulled out the frog from her pocket and handed him to Alice.

"Don't tell me... this is Peter?" she teased.

"No. Just some guard who tried to rape me before," Katrina said. "But that's not important. I heard Lion order the captain to have everyone killed by Friday."

"Everyone? But how could they do that?" Alice asked. "You know they just meant the Jews."

"No. He asked that. She said everyone. She said she wants no one to be here come Friday and they have to start tomorrow."

"But how?" Alice held onto the frog. "Could we eat him?" she asked. The frog wiggled, but it didn't get him free.

"Eat him, I don't care. They want to put us into gas chambers, fifty at a time," Katrina said. "We could be dead tomorrow, or the day after."

"Then it's time," Alice said.

"Yes. It's time for us to leave this place and never return," Katrina agreed.

The rest of the night, the two girls plotted just how they would leave.

CHAPTER TWENTY-THREE

The next morning, Alice and Katrina were tired. Planning their escape, they barely slept. They hoped their plan would work before it was their turn to go into the chambers with the others. That thought made their bodies shiver.

Alice had just finished her chores and was walking back to her tent. She saw Peter walking towards her. Katrina had been hoping to see him and explain, but he was great at hiding and avoiding her. "I need to speak to you, Sir," Alice said. She bowed which was something she had never done before. He looked down at her for the first time. Days before, they would tease each other about the dumbest things. It was amazing how much things can change with just the single word "Witch."

"What about, Jew?" he said. The word made Alice blink hard. She held her hands closed to avoid turning him into a lizard or a frog like Katrina had done to the guard the night before.

"My name is Alice and you know that. Please call me by my name. I need to talk to you about Katrina and the fight you had right before her aunt died." Alice knew she should not tell him their plan just yet. Katrina would tell him herself when the time was right.

Peter's shoulders slumped. "How is she recovering from that? I tried to get Lion to give her the medicine, but she wouldn't. She was being evil."

"Katrina's heartbroken because she lost two people in less than twenty-four hours."

"I'm heartbroken too," Peter said. His eyes looked

sad. His whole body looked starved for love. He seemed to miss Katrina more than he wanted to admit. "You're a witch too?" He whispered.

Alice looked around the area to make sure no one was listening to them. She gave a soft nod and continued to talk. "Just because we're witches, it doesn't mean we're bad."

"But she lied to me," Peter said. His eyes became watery.

"Only to protect you. Only to keep you safe. She made me promise not to hurt you or use my powers on you," Alice said. "And trust me, that was hard, especially after you had that fight with her." She laughed.

Peter let a slight smile creep across his face. "But..."

"Do you love Katrina?"

Peter nodded.

"Then don't worry about her magic powers. Be concerned with the magic of your true love," Alice said. "You should have been there when her aunt died. You knew how much that woman meant to Katrina. Why weren't you there?"

"Because I couldn't be!" Peter said.

"You could have. You were just too afraid to be there. You didn't know what to expect."

"You're right." Peter looked down. "I really love her."

"Then go tell her that. She's in the mess hall, I think." Alice walked off. "If you make her cry again, I will turn you into a frog," she called from behind her.

Peter smiled knowing that Alice could and would do it too. He ran to the mess hall. He didn't want to miss his chance to speak to her. Katrina was behind the counters helping the women clean. She tried to help the older sick prisoners as much as she could.

"I need to talk to you," Peter said. He was panting from having run so fast to get there.

"Okay." She placed the rag down then gave the three women a hug before drying her hands and walking out with Peter.

"I talked to Alice," Peter said. He pulled Katrina close and before she could say anything, his lips were on top of hers. They were kissing in the middle of the camp. Guards whistled and children giggled at them. Neither of them cared or bothered to stop. They kept kissing as if they had been apart for years. "I love you more now that I know your secret," he whispered.

"I never stopped loving you," Katrina said. She looked deep into his eyes and saw a future in them. His amazing soul was bright and something she wanted to experience every day for the rest of her life. Then suddenly she remembered last night. She remembered Lion and the captain talking. "I need to show you something," she whispered. She grabbed his hand and intertwined her fingers into his. Then she led him to her tent.

"What is it?" said Peter.

"They're going to kill us," she said. "And it starts today."

Peter shook his head. "No they aren't. They couldn't." His jaw tensed and he touched her hand. "I won't let them do that to you or Alice."

"Thank you, Peter. I knew you'd feel that way, but it's not something you can control. I wish you could. I wish I had enough power to control it, but I don't." Katrina lowered her head and sighed deeply. "I heard Lion talking last night to the captain. She plans to kill us all."

"Maybe you misunderstood." Peter tried to reassure her, but it didn't work.

"I can show you." Katrina remembered when her father would show her memories of her grandparents. "Touch my hand," she said. Peter swallowed hard, not knowing what to expect. "I won't hurt you," she said.

He placed his hand into hers. "Okay," he said. He was nervous, but as he felt the warmness of her fingers in his, his anxiousness eased.

"Close your eyes and focus on my hand," she said. She closed her eyes and began to hum as she slowly remembered the evening before. She placed her mind back at the tent.

"Oh, wow," Peter whispered as he heard and saw everything Katrina had the night before. He saw his uncle talking to Lion. He could hear the fear in his uncle's voice. He could hear the evil inside of Lion. "Wow," Peter kept saying, until Katrina finally pulled her fingers away. She made sure she did this before the guard approached her and tried to take advantage of her.

"Do you believe me now?" Katrina asked.

"I do. But what can we do about it?" Peter asked.

"Alice and I planned an escape for tonight. You can come with us. You must come with us. We could use your strength and experience."

"But are you sure you want me there?" Peter teased. He pulled her close and pressed his lips on hers for a split second. "You can't keep me from escaping with you," he said. "Plus, I have special access to the gates in the front of the camp. And, I know the way around the forest, so you won't run into all the dangers that are there.

"Then we need to get Alice in here to figure out how to do this without getting caught, or hurt, or killed." Katrina got up and was about to run out. "But first, I want to say I'm sorry for lying to you."

"I do understand. Alice explained to me why you lied. I had to think about it and realized she's right. You would have been killed the moment you arrived here had you said you were a witch in the Resistance."

"I'm glad you understand. I'm going to go get Alice."

"Katrina. Wait. One question." Peter said.

"Yes?"

"There's a guard that's been missing since late last night," said Peter. "We've been looking for him and can't find him."

"He's still alive," Katrina smiled. "I turned him into a frog after he tried to rape me last night."

"Okay," Peter said. "I would have killed him."

"Alice will bring him with her. I think he's still in her pocket." Katrina raced off to find Alice.

Peter couldn't help but laugh. He'd have to prepare for this kind of talk if he was going to marry Katrina. And, he was definitely going to marry her. This meant he'd have to be prepared for the witch talk.

CHAPTER TWENTY-FOUR

The evening was long, but night finally fell upon them. Katrina was lost in her thoughts and fears. There was no point in avoiding it all. The sound of a small bell went off in the distance. This was the cue that it was time to go. Although she barely slept the night before, she felt wide-awake.

Her eyes widened as she remembered the events from a few nights ago.

"Have you seen my daughter?" a young mother said. She asked all over the camp. It wasn't until the mother saw the bodies being taken from the gas chamber that she realized her daughter was in the pile. There is no telling how the child even got into the chamber group, but she was gone.

It broke Katrina's heart.

It made Alice angry. She didn't want any of this to happen. She wished she had the strength to bring the dead back to life, but the last thing they needed was zombies all over the camp. For now, she wouldn't focus on things she could do nothing about. Instead, she had to focus on getting out of this hell and, with luck, sending help back for the others.

Katrina poked Alice. Alice slowly woke up. It amazed Katrina that Alice could sleep, no matter what was going on.

"No more innocent people will be killed at this camp after we leave," Alice said the moment she woke up. "When we leave, we have to return with the Resistance and get the prisoners help before it's too late."

"We will. We will. I promise we will do just that," Katrina said. "But we have to get out of here fast then. It's crazy quiet for some reason."

Katrina could hear the breathing of the girls and women in the tent with them. Katrina and Alice didn't even hear the sound of guard walking outside. No depressing sounds of girls being raped or children being spanked for whatever reason. No sound of bricks breaking. Nothing. It was deadly quiet and it didn't seem right. Alice and Katrina had been through so much in this place, they couldn't hold back their pain any longer. Katrina felt like she was walking on a tight rope over a lake of fire. They only had one more lake of fire to cross before the gates to heaven opened and they were safe from harm.

"So, tell me the plan again," Alice thought to Katrina.

"We're going to meet Peter near the gate. He'll have the key code to unlock it so we can get out," Katrina thought back.

"Are you sure this is a good idea? What if we're caught and killed?" Alice swallowed hard. I wish your aunt was here to come with us." Tears fell from her eyes.

Katrina started to cry too, but she held back. She wouldn't let herself sob or get too bogged down in sadness. "We can't think like that right now. We have to get out of here before it's too late." She grabbed Alice by the hand. "We'll be killed here or out there. But we...at least...we have to fight for ourselves."

"Then let's just do this," Alice said. They raced out of the tent where they had been sleeping for just over five weeks. In five weeks, they had lost everything that mattered to them, but found each other. In five weeks, they had learned to use their magic and be powerful, while helping as many people as possible. They were not the same young witches who had come into the camp, fearing they'd be killed if they did something wrong or for no reason at all. They had become sisters, powerful sisters.

Standing in the grounds, near the gate was Peter. He walked around in a small circle, waiting. He looked nervous. He had a large backpack slung over his shoulder. Peter smiled the moment he saw them. Katrina felt her cheeks heat up. She wasn't sure if it was because she and Peter would be alone soon, or because she was hot with rage and energy.

Peter looked all around the camp. Finally, he whispered, "There are no guards out here. I guess we really did get lucky. There's usually at least a couple at this time. Still, we need to be on the lookout."

Katrina and Alice nodded. They went to the front gate. There was a locked door with a keypad under the handle. Peter approached the keypad, typed in the code, and inserted the key into the keyhole close to the pad.

At first, nothing happened. The three of them stood there sweating. Their breaths were short and quick. They waited and hoped it would work. Peter's fingers began to tremble. He knew they needed to be super quiet, otherwise he would have begun to yell and curse in German. They all knew that if the code was wrong, an alarm would sound and wake the whole camp.

Click! The door swung open and Peter led them through it. They each took a deep breath and released it slowly. They relaxed for the first time in weeks. It seemed surreal. Katrina reached to pinch herself hoping she would wake up if it were a dream. Thankfully, she felt the pain.

Surrounding them was a massive, thick forest. In the far distance, Katrina could see mountains and smoke coming from them. She opened her arms out wide and looked up at the sky. The moon was only a small little thumbnail size, but she loved it. "I miss you Auntie," she whispered.

Alice looked back at the camp as she stepped forward. They each expected an alarm to go off with a huge red alert. They expected something different to happen. She didn't think it would be this easy. As they walked deeper into the woods, her mind wasn't thinking about whether or not she would be dead before the next night; it focused on how soon the

Resistance could save the hundreds of other women and children that were still in the camp. Her heart nearly beat out of her chest. But, it wasn't the same kind of beating it had done when she came to Camp Ravensbrook on a bus filled with other Jews who were all scared they were going to be killed. The heartbeat was from excitement and most importantly freedom.

Suddenly, there was a sound. It sounded like lots of footsteps moving closer and closer towards them. Instead of the sound coming from the camp, it came from the woods themselves. Katrina held onto Alice's hand. She tried to reach for Peter, but he was too far ahead of them and too distracted to notice.

"What?" Peter cried, in German.

Guards who should have been at their posts in the camp sprung from the woods. Peter glared at them. Then someone else came out from the woods. They saw her high heels first. She walked towards them. It was Lion. Instead of her normal outfit, she wore a black dress with knee high boots. She still wore the bright red lipstick and red hair, along with her long pointed cat nails. Katrina couldn't help think that she appeared younger than she really was.

This was the first time Katrina had ever seen her so close. Katrina held back her anger at that moment by balling her hand into a fist. She thought it best to wait for the chance to run free and leave this place forever.

"You thought I wouldn't know," said Lion. Her voice showed only malice, strong enough to bore holes into the tree trunks around them. She smirked. "Like I'm really that stupid."

Katrina and Alice looked at Peter. He was just as confused as they were. What was Lion talking about?

"I couldn't believe it at first," said Lion. "I thought by now all the guards in this stupid worthless camp were under my control. But, it seems you resisted my control, Peter. Maybe some basic magic will work on you instead!" Lion pointed her long finger at Peter and began to wave it. "Go ahead and do a dance for me little boy." She teased and taunted. The magic didn't work though. Peter just stood there with his eyes wide open, not knowing what to think or say. "How can you not be affected by my magic?"

"How is it you have magic in the first place?" Alice asked.

Lion gritted her teeth. "Do you really think you're the only witch in this camp? Do you really think you have a right to talk to me that way? I'm going to be the ruler of this miserable country some day and you will be my slaves." Pointing to Alice, she said, "I work with the Germans to rid the world of Jews like you." Then she looked at Katrina. "I remember you. You begged me for that medicine to cure your dying aunt." She began to laugh. "It was so worthless for you to cry. At first, I didn't realize you were a witch. You seemed so human. I decided to let you be. Then, the other night I saw you turn that guard into a frog and it was all I needed to go ahead with my plan." She pointed at Katrina. "I'm going to make people all over the world my servants. They will do as I say. I will be rich, powerful, and in complete control of everything and everybody. And I think I'll start with you little girl."

"I would run if I were you. These girls are more powerful then you will ever be." Peter finally got his voice back.

Lion pulled her finger up and jerked it forward. Peter was flung into the trunk of a nearby tree. Katrina ran to his side to make sure he was okay. He was still breathing but his eyes were closed and there was a deep cut on the top of his head.

"Why would you want to do this to your own kind? Don't you have any kind of soul?" Alice asked her.

"You should understand that the Resistance will win this war!"

Lion burst out laughing. "I'm not a part of the Resistance. I want to be the ruler of this world. If I'm the ruler, I decide everything. I want to be in charge. The one who everyone bows down to and everyone cries to about their dead families. I want to be the woman who rules the earth and the afterlife. Without stupid little girls like you two, I can do just that!"

Katrina shook her fist as she stood up. She couldn't just stand there while this woman said such evil things and had such evil plans. The death of her parents, the death of her aunt, the suffering she endured, all because of Nazis Germany and this insane woman. Her entire body began glowing. A greenish aura appeared around her. Lion started clapping once again. She hadn't noticed the glowing or that Katrina was getting more and more angry.

"So you two are the ones who have been causing trouble around this camp. You two have been saving women and children from this hell. Stopping me from spreading my red liquid all over the world. This is very interesting. No matter. I'll put an end to all of you within a few seconds. Guards, apprehend them!"

The army of guards charged, each brandishing their weapons. Katrina grabbed Alice's hand and they both began glowing. The two witches stuck out their palms. Never had they felt so powerful. Their combined power was better than anything they had ever felt before.

A massive wave of energy shot from them. All the guards flew back. Some crashed into trees, others fell on top of one another. Lion shielded her eyes, her dress flapping. Other than that, she was the only one not affected. All the guards were out cold.

Instead of showing fear, Lion laughed. "Ha. Pretty good. You two, once I capture you, will be experimented on, that's for sure. Maybe I could harness your power. I'm sure the doctor would love placing your heads into a cabinet to be shown to everyone."

The glowing surrounding Katrina and Alice stopped. "Are you still blabbering?" said Katrina. "We have enough power to knock out all your guards, so why aren't you running?"

Lion chuckled. A dark flame emerged from her palm. She held it and stared at the two girls. "Because even though you two have power, I still have enough power in my pinky to take you out."

Katrina and Alice tried casting a spell, but before they could, Lion shot a dark flame from her hand. It stretched to form a rope made of fire and chased them like a snake about to strike. It wrapped around the two of them, constricting their bodies. The flame felt surprisingly cold. Katrina's teeth chattered.

"See? You won't be able to break from those flames." Lion's eyes blazed. "If you don't surrender now, the rope will freeze your bodies."

"Katrina!" Peter shouted. He woke up just in time to see the hell that was happening only steps from him. He ran to help Katrina and Alice. But, Lion pointed her finger at him again. He fell back to the ground and was unconscious.

"Quiet, you. Now then, will you two surrender and volunteer to be my tiny little mice, or will you die now? Your decision."

Katrina looked at Alice. "Just give up!" Alice screamed at Lion.

Katrina felt the freezing temperatures slowing down her movements, but the fire burning in her soul kept her warm. This woman was responsible for all that happened in Camp Ravensbrook. She wasn't going to get away with it. Katrina could hear her mother call from the other side, telling her to remember the love. She could hear her father pointing out just how to take Lion's powers. She could even hear her aunt saying prayers and giving her more strength than she had ever felt before. Her mind was free.

A new aura surrounded Katrina's body, this one golden. It grew wider and brighter. Alice's mouth dropped. Katrina looked at Peter's body. The aura grew bigger. "You will pay for this!" Katrina screamed.

The flames holding the girls prisoners exploded into nothingness. Lion clapped. "Very impressive," she said.

Katrina rushed towards Lion, who opened up her palm. "Bad move," Lion declared. A blast of magic shot from her palm, its power was enough to destroy every atom in a person's body.

But, it never hit Katrina. The beam passed Alice and Peter and finally hit a tree. When the beam disappeared, there was a crater where the tree stood. It could have killed Katrina if it hit her.

Lion stood with her mouth open wide. She didn't see Katrina move behind her. Katrina's golden aura concentrated in her fist. Lion turned around, but it was too late.

Lightning shot from Katrina's fist, piercing Lion with one thick bolt. The evil witch flew back, her body convulsing. The aura around Katrina disappeared and she began feeling lightheaded. Using that much-concentrated magic caused her to suffer from magic fatigue. She wouldn't be able to attack again or defend herself. Thankfully, it seemed that Lion was down. She lay on her face, not moving.

Alice ran to Katrina and gave her a hug. "Let's go!" she cried.

"Help me with Peter," Katrina told her.

The witches rushed towards the tree. Katrina shook

Peter's body. At first, he seemed dead.

"Peter!" Katrina cried out. There was no response. This woman could not take away her love too, could she? Tears fell from her eyes as she held his face in her hands. She kissed his forehead. "Peter wake up. I love you too much to let you go." Finally, he began to stir in her arms.

Alice smiled as she watched Katrina bend over and kiss him his cheek softly.

"I love you too much too," he said. He was still groggy.

"We have to get going in case she wakes up," Katrina said. She began to help him up. He seemed to have a broken leg. If she remembered a spell for broken legs she would have said it, but her memory was blank for the moment.

Alice and Katrina helped Peter walk. As they passed Lion, there was a stirring. Katrina turned around.

"Down!" Katrina shouted. The trio ducked.

Lion jerked her body up, looking at Katrina and Alice with ice in her eyes. Another blast shot from her hand. It missed them by less than an inch.

"Why won't you both just die?" Lion stood up. Her body wobbled and her clothes were in tatters.

"Because we don't give up," Katrina shouted.

"You have enough left?" Alice thought to Katrina.

"We'll have to do this one together," Katrina thought back.

They held hands and looked at Lion. This time, Lion had the same emotions many of the prisoners had whenever a guard attacked them. Lion tried backing away. She tried firing her spells, but nothing came out.

Another golden aura exploded from Katrina and Alice and this time, it flashed in many colors.

"Don't!" Lion screamed. "I'll shut down the camp!"

The girls knew it was an empty promise and it was already too late. A flashing wave of magic shot from Katrina and Alice's bodies. Lion tried running, but the wave overtook her. Colors flashed all around and over Lion.

When it cleared, Lion was still standing. She walked towards the girls, cackling as she did. Katrina and Alice stood firm.

"Looks like your spell didn't work," said Lion. "And, now you're all pooped out! I'm going to have fun with you two."

She stuck out her palm. Peter dove toward the girls to protect them. But, nothing came out of Lion. "Why isn't my magic working?" she cried.

"We accomplished what you tried so hard to do. We took away all of your magic," Katrina told her.

"That's impossible!" Lion shouted. As she shouted at the witches, her voice became hoarse. Her red hair changed to white. Wrinkles cracked her face. She was soon a very old lady and fell to the ground.

"We'll send the Resistance to gather your bones and free the women and children too," Peter said.

EPILOGUE

Three Years Later

The London weather was perfect that afternoon. Katrina's long black hair moved with the wind. The chill felt nice on her face. She smiled nearly every minute of the day. She hadn't thought of being killed for a long time. Life improved after they escaped Camp Ravensbrook. They went to fight with the Resistance. After six long months of witch fighting, the Americans came and helped them defeat the Nazis military. Their combined efforts finally put an end to the evil war that had haunted the world for way too long.

Now, Katrina sat outside, resting on the balcony of her home. She looked out and watched the beauty of London all around her. She wasn't small and thin, or dirty. Instead, she had a stomach from all the London dishes she had been eating. There was nothing like actually eating sweet breads and tasting every bite of it, instead of just wishing she were eating it. It was freedom.

Behind her sat three bassinets. In them were her triplets. Her mother always said that she wished there were three Katrinas around the home, because she was so special there should have been more than one of her. And, there they were... three versions of herself. Three identical girls covered in lace and love. They weren't being raised in a place where they would be hated for being different. Instead, they would be shown the best form of love. They were only a few weeks old and already they were the light of Katrina's life and her whole world. She felt blessed to have a job that allowed her to be a mom first and an artist second.

In her lap sat a book. Within that book, her drawings. She was the woman in the town who restored old paintings for the many museums. In her spare time, she would draw things that came to her. Today it was the image of her family. She placed her mother on one side, her aunt on the other, and her father in the center. On the bottom of them, she placed flowers and a sweet spell that she would hear her father say at times when making stars for her mother. Not a day went by when her mind wouldn't drift to them. She missed them dearly. She was glad to be alive of course, but she wished her family was there to share in the beauty of life.

"Honey," Peter called from the kitchen. His voice a small whisper. Life had changed so much for him as well. From a soldier to a businessman in the middle of the city. Peter was no longer bossed around, instead he was the boss. He controlled a factory that made dolls and toy trains. Each one priceless and handmade with love by the hands of women who cared about quality. He loved his job and was excited to share his favorite dolls with his young children. "Breakfast is ready," he added quickly.

Katrina placed the book on the chair and tiptoed past her sleeping children. One of them, Alley began to stir, but thankfully didn't wake up. She walked up to Peter and wrapped her arms around his neck. She pulled him close and into a deep passionate kiss. For years, they could enjoy each other without restrictions. It was awesome. "Did I tell you how much I love you yet today?" she asked.

"Nope." Peter laughed lightly. "And, I sure do love when you say it." He added a soft kiss on her forehead before picking her up. He hugged her tight.

"Let's eat, silly man," she said. "Alice and Johny will be here shortly," she added with a hint of excitement. It made all three of their girls wake up. Peter and Katrina went to their daughters. "Breakfast for five this time!" she added. She lifted Martha from the bassinet. Peter took Alley and Lily out and placed them gently onto his lap as he sat down.

Magic was a normal part of the day. Katrina was able to use the very tip of her finger to serve their meal, while they held the babies. It made daily home life less challenging.

An hour later, Alice was knocking on their front door with a purple iris in her hands and a husband standing beside her. She had only just gotten married three months ago. She still held the first year of marriage glow on her face, along with the passion in her eyes that proved she loved the man she stood next to.

"Come in!" Katrina said hugging her friend. "You have to see my sweethearts. They've grown so." There was no point in hiding the excitement. Katrina talked to Alice every other day. They were best friends, after all. It was an endless friendship.

Alice walked in wearing a bright flower covered yellow and pink dress. It hugged her much nicer than the ugly outfits they wore in the camp. She had her hair tied up in a bun on top of her head and bright pink lipstick on her plump lips. She wore large earrings and even a pearl necklace she had found in the rubble of her burnt home after the war ended. She had the glow of being happy. There were no worries about being Jewish.

Her husband was strong as a tiger and just as quiet. He was easy going and a few years older than Alice and Katrina. He had a deep voice to match his age. Johny was younger than Peter, however. He was smart and could debate for hours about history with Peter, if their wives gave them the chance.

Alice married Johny and the two of them owned a restaurant right in the middle of downtown. They spent their evenings testing recipes and feeding each other until they were too full to walk. It was the best way to live when there were no children. Children would be part of their plans for the next year or two. The newlyweds still had plenty of time to have their own set of triplets.

Alice met Johny when she went back to finish high school after the war. It was love at first sight for them both. Johny planned on becoming a soldier after he finished high school, but his love for Alice kept him home. He did though spend weekends volunteering at the fire department when time allowed. It was a perfect match for the two of them, since they both were witches.

They enjoyed owning a restaurant where they could showcase their amazing talents for great dishes. Johny created American dishes and Alice was able to prepare all the Jewish and German dishes she grew up with. It made a truly perfect place to eat.

The two couples ate, talked and laughed for the next few hours. They talked about everything from the present, to the future, and of course the past.

"Life has so many changes, right?" Katrina said holding onto Peter's hand. She couldn't help but become teary eyed at the memory of it all.

"And, I'm happy about every single one of them," said Alice. "Without us, the war would have gone on." And, she was right of course. She often mourned the death of her family and even the death of Katrina's Aunt Lisa.

"Without magic you mean." Peter laughed. "Without magic I would never be with this amazing woman next to me and have those three beautiful daughters." He leaned forward and kissed Katrina's check.

"To the Resistance," Katrina said lifting her glass into the air. The glasses clanked. Never had she felt so at peace. It was a 'peace' that felt like it would last for a lifetime and then some.

THANK YOU

Thank you for reading my book. If you enjoyed it, please take a moment to leave me a review.

ABOUT THE AUTHOR

R. T. Johnson was born in Des Moines, Iowa, but currently resides in Denver, Colorado. He graduated from the University of Phoenix with a degree in business administration. He served for more than 30 years with the Air National Guard. He retired from the Los Angeles County probation service, where he helped minors adjust their lifestyles and turn their lives around. He has been married for 40 years to his wonderful wife—between them they have more than 80 years of serving people.

Connect with R. T. Johnson at this website:

http://childrensfantasyadventurebooks.com/

Printed in Great Britain
by Amazon